Ex Libris

AT
HOME
WITH
CRAZY
Katrina Martin

MILFLORES

At Home with Crazy
Katrina I. Martin

Copyright © 2022 Katrina I. Martin

Published and exclusively distributed by
Milflores Publishing, Inc.
1244 E. Amang Rodriguez Avenue
De La Paz, Pasig City 1600
Philippines
info@milflorespublishing.com
www.milflorespublishing.com

National Library of the Philippines CIP Data

Recommended entry:

Martin, Katrina I.
At home with crazy / Katrina I. Martin. — Pasig City :
Milflores Publishing Inc., [2022], ©2022.
Pages ; cm

ISBN 978-971-828-122-2

1. Family — Fiction. 2. Friendship — Fiction.

3. Philippine fiction (English) I. Title.

899.210355   PR9550.9.M37   2022   P220220105

Cover artwork by Angela Taguiang

Cover and Book design by Mikke Gallardo

For my parents, my siblings,
and Anna and Cayt

MOM V. ZOMBIE

Today I knew that Mom would be our mom again.

The scent of melting tablea, like chocolate infused with bitter coffee, wafted through our bedroom door. The pure cacao was used to make Sam's and my favorite chocolate rice porridge, and it had always been Mom who made us that dish. That could only mean that she was having a good day and that the rest of us would have one too.

Good days in our family had been few and far in between the past year, so I knew better than to waste them by lying in bed streaming movies, which I could do any other time, especially now that we had moved to a city with slightly better internet.

I threw aside the covers and hurtled down the now-familiar spiral staircase in our new apartment. When I reached the landing, I heard Mom's voice coming from the kitchen.

"Don't forget your sister."

Oops.

"I didn't!" I yelled as I tiptoe-ran on my way back to our room.

"Sam, hurry up! Breakfast," I said as I shook Sam's tiny shoulders, her head practically flopping back and forth. She murmured and turned her back towards me. What the grownups say is true: people who weren't sleeping were much harder to wake up.

I parted Sam's curly black hair and blew into her left ear. On cue, my sister started giggling.

"Come on, Mom made *champorado*," I said, patting her on the butt.

Sam's head shot out of her bed like I had just recited a magic word. She began sniffing, her tiny nose up in the air like a little puppy's. I started towards the stairs again, confident that the shuffling sounds that followed meant that Sam was right behind me. We clambered down in our bedroom slippers, noisily announcing our descent to our parents.

"Thought you zombies were never gonna rise from the dead. I was about to go in and turn off the air conditioning," Dad said, looking up from his newspaper as we walked into the kitchen.

"I'm actually shocked you didn't already do that," I teased.

"Well, I thought you girls deserved a treat. It is your last day of summer vacation, after all," Dad said, grinning so wide that his eyes practically disappeared under his square, horn-rimmed glasses.

"Yeah, right," Mom retorted, her back towards us as she kept cooking. "I had to barricade their bedroom door to keep you from doing just that."

"Ha! Knew it." I laughed. Dad was always gonna be Dad.

"Waste not, want not, girls. Valuable life lesson right there," Dad said, reaching from under the paper to tousle Sam's curly hair. My sister beamed at him. Then Dad shifted his hand to grab a strip of bacon from the bowl that Mom had just set on the table next to a platter of fried eggs and dried fish. Mom's hand snatched it even before Dad could take his first bite.

"Uh-uh. You're such a bad example."

"Who, me?" Dad pretended to be shocked as Mom took the seat next to him. As she leaned forward to give me and Sam generous portions of everything, the yellow kitchen light illuminated Mom's face, highlighting the cheekbones that subtly rose from under her dark brown eyes. Her lips curved into a warm smile as she looked at me.

It was like staring at my reflection in a mirror. But it wasn't just that we shared the same eyes with barely any lid, flat noses, thin lips, and a lot of tiny moles on our faces. Rather, Mom looked the way I felt at this moment, which was pretty darn happy.

"After breakfast, you girls need to *at least* open your books," Mom began to say. "Tomorrow's the first day of classes! The curriculum in Lorenzo will be more advanced than in your old schools in Cauayan. And oh my, Sam! It'll be your first time to go to class in person too."

I know other people would've rolled their eyes at their mother's nagging but, as dorky as it sounds, I think I kinda missed that. I sure preferred it over me having to nag Sam. My little sister hardly ever obeyed me so I often ended up having to do her share of the chores too. But with Mom calling the shots, it was a different story.

And Mom did have a point: the first day of school *was* a big deal. Sam and I had spent the better part of the last few years locked up at home and attending classes online, thanks to a nasty pandemic that basically made it dangerous for people to gather in large groups or hang around each other without wearing face masks. It was kinda like being in a movie about a zombie apocalypse, which would've been cool, except millions of people around the world just stayed dead instead of resurrecting into flesh-eating monsters.

"—That means no locking yourself upstairs rewatching horror movies or whatever the heck it is you do, Cayt," Mom continued, interrupting my thoughts.

I chuckled inwardly, thinking 1) Zombie movies weren't necessarily horror films; 2) I wasn't rewatching movies but trying to find inspiration for a new video for my channel; and 3) maybe I didn't miss the nagging that much. Mom wouldn't be so dismissive if I were watching *Eternal Sunshine of the Gormless*

Brain or whatever her boring, supposedly sophisticated favorites were called. But I guess I should be happy that Mom is normal today, even if that meant she'd be frowning upon my life choices and making me do things I didn't want to do. Isn't that what adults were for anyway?

"Heck!" Sam laughed. She looked so delighted with herself for saying what she thought was a naughty word. Oh, to be young and stupid!

I saw Dad give Sam his best stern look and chuckled again. Walking past the pigsty at the family farm back in Cauayan was five times more threatening than the face Dad puts on when he's trying to discipline us.

"*Heck* isn't a word you say just for the fun of it, Sam, you know that."

"It's not a curse word, Dad," I defended. I was going to add that most of the shows Sam and I watched used far more explicit language, but I stopped myself just in time before he could think of locking us out of his Netflix account.

"Listen to your father, you two. Wait, what the—? Shoot!"

Mom hurried to turn off the stove. The faint smell of burnt chocolate lingered in the air.

"*Champorado's* ready," Dad said. Sam and I giggled as Mom hurled a pot holder at him.

Yup. Today was definitely going to be a good day.

Wanting to go along with Mom's rare good mood, Sam and I spent most of the day *trying* to read our books. Operative word: trying. Every time I started on a math equation, I would doze off and dream about an odd-looking zombie in a house dress barging into the room and tearing my book apart before running after me. After what seemed like the third dream, I woke up with drool on my left cheek and an idea for my next project at last: Family moves into a new house post-apocalypse, not knowing it's haunted by a child-eating zombie. Classic!

I grabbed the sketchpad from underneath my Math textbook and seated myself at my favorite spot in Sam's and my shared new room: the built-in bench under the wide windows overlooking the street. I drew four boxes on the page and, inside the last one, started sketching a rotting hand emerging from within a dark doorway and latching onto the bottom of the doorframe. Then I started filling in the first three boxes with moving-in scenes.

I chewed on the end of my pencil as I recalled memories from when our family first arrived at this row of narrow, two-storey gray units called Elvira Apartments just two weeks ago.

We had pulled up along a sleepy Cordillera street in the middle of the night after making a right turn from a busy thoroughfare. *Jeepneys* and buses and cars still hummed in the distance, their tail lights blinking red and yellow under a wild tapestry of electric lines. Then Dad, Sam, and I alighted our SUV and were greeted by our landlady-to-be, an elderly woman in a housedress and hair rollers. She had a face mask over her mouth, but I could tell she was smiling by the way the outer corners of her eyes slanted downwards as she spoke.

My arms were still sore from when Sam and I had helped Dad drag over a dozen bags and boxes from the trunk and into our new apartment while Mom stayed seated inside the car, absentmindedly dangling her legs from out the open door. It was only when our landlady was about to retire to her apartment that Mom finally moved and chose that very moment to hum a graduation march animatedly and in perfect tune for reasons unknown to the rest of us.

I winced. Well that won't fit into my story.

I made a mental note to *not* depend on Mom to contribute to this project in any way. If the past months had taught me anything, it was that there was absolutely no telling how long her being Mom-like would last. This would just have to be a simple short film about a single dad and daughter moving into an apartment with a zombie. No biggie. Indie filmmakers had to work with cast and crew limitations all the time. When the pandemic first broke out, the great Filipino-Russian filmmaker

Harriette Swarog wrote, directed, shot, edited, and performed a Netflix special all by herself in some tiny studio in Palawan. And it was a masterpiece.

I flipped the page and began drawing more boxes. But before I could start on the next scene, Mom was already calling on us from downstairs and telling me and Sam to get ready for church.

Dad was in such high spirits after Sunday mass that, instead of going straight home afterwards, he decided we should go to the mall and eat dinner out—which *never* happens, not even in our old town. Not even pre-pandemic.

Inside the car, my eyes darted between my parents, who were both laughing contentedly at some joke Sam had just made about seatbelts. Mom was all smiles and Dad was not acting like the world's biggest cheapskate for once. It felt weird but in a good way. Like moving had allowed us to leave behind the unpleasant things that had happened in the last year and just start fresh.

It was only a short drive to Fisher Mall, which Dad said was called that because it supposedly had the freshest fish you could find in a supermarket. I laughed at the thought of stepping into an air-conditioned wet market, with vendors bullying you into buying king crabs and giant tuna. But when we arrived, Fisher Mall seemed pretty normal, just a bigger version of what we had in Cauayan, though still small by Manila standards. That was alright. Big malls could get pretty tiring especially when all our parents allowed us to do was window shop anyway.

Then again, big malls made it less likely for you to bump into someone you knew too. But I was almost certain that the probability of that happening here was near zero. If I had any other schoolmates from Cauayan who would be studying or vacationing in Manila, I was pretty sure they would rather visit the fancier malls. I mean, did Fisher even have a Starbucks? I had no idea.

I looked at Dad, whistling like a schoolboy as he walked beside Mom, his hand holding hers, and wondered if he had the same intentions for choosing this place. Aside from spending less money on gas, I had a feeling Dad wasn't in a hurry to meet somebody from home either. Though it was probably more out of concern for Mom than for his own reputation.

To be honest, I hated sneaking around as if we were the last humans in a city swarming with flesh-eating monsters. But keeping to ourselves all the time was even more frustrating, especially after being stuck at home for over two years. It was about time we went out again. How bad could it be?

We stopped by the grocery to stock up on pantry essentials. Mom seemed pretty surprised that I knew which items, brands, and sizes to get for most things. I bit my lip so I wouldn't accidentally tell her that, while she had been hibernating in her room for days on end like a vampire (not the *Twilight* kind), I had been doing the grocery shopping back in Cauayan with Ate Fe and my Lola every other week for the last half year or so.

After our quick detour to the supermarket, our parents let us choose where we wanted to get dinner. I bribed Sam to vote for a Korean grill in exchange for doing her dishes for a week, which I usually did anyway. Aside from my samgyupsal craving, I wanted to eat there because it wasn't as crowded as the other places we had passed by—perfect for staying under the radar. From outside, I could see that only two tables were occupied—one by an elderly couple, and another by a trio of young women, one of them with vivid aquamarine hair that for some reason reminded me of mermaids—and none of them young enough to be potential classmates. But then I took one glance at the menu and knew why. I watched my dad's nose twitch as he scanned it "Chinese-style," which meant looking at the prices first and then settling for whatever fit your budget. But really, I don't know why Filipinos don't just call it "Ilocano-style." It kinda meant the same thing.

After spending ten minutes agonizing over the menu, Dad finally asked for a table. Before he could change his mind, I grabbed Sam who, up until then had been pirouetting (at least, that's what I thought she was attempting to do) from one end of the hallway to the other. We sat at a corner table and were soon after served a plate of raw beef, pork, and chicken to grill. Mom and I really enjoyed wrapping the grilled meat in lettuce and adding kimchi sprouts or zucchini slices. Sam looked like she was enjoying testing Dad's patience while he taught her how to use the chopsticks.

I challenged Sam to see if she could transfer five slices of chicken into her bowl, taking videos of her attempts using my phone. For some reason, viewing things through a camera always made me feel better. I had also listened to a podcast about how Harriette Swarog would rewatch real footage of normal events to help her write scenes, and thought I should build up my own library too. I stifled my laughter and steadied my hands while recording Sam, the meat constantly slipping from between her chopsticks.

As we wolfed down our food, I noticed that people had started trickling into the restaurant and that almost every table was occupied just thirty minutes after we had sat down to eat. Next to our booth, a young couple with a stroller had just been seated. Their server returned to them with a high chair on which the dad secured the baby, a little boy that looked like an overstuffed doll with wisps of brown hair on his tiny head.

It was adorable how he laughed whenever his mom spooned mush into his mouth, cooing "good boy" after each bite.

The baby had me in a trance. Until I felt a sharp and sticky rap on my forehead.

"What the—? Sam!"

My sister had just tapped me on the forehead using the oily end of her chopsticks. Gross.

"You're not looking," Sam accused me as she held chopsticks over her bowl of rice, which now had exactly five slices of chicken at the top.

"How do I know you didn't just sneak those in with your fingers? You should do one more," I dared Sam as I redirected my gaze towards her. Out of the corner of my eye, I noticed how Mom was only just turning her attention away from the baby too.

"Take a video for evidence," Sam ordered, waving the chopsticks in the air as if it were a magic wand. I took my phone and obliged.

"Careful, hun," Dad said absent-mindedly. I shifted the camera towards him just as he was stuffing a particularly large lettuce wrap into his mouth. *Fry nuffoo frop anyfing.*

"Huh?" Sam looked up at Dad with her forehead all wrinkled up.

Dad nearly choked trying to swallow that last bit. His voice hoarse, he said, "Try not to drop anything."

"What Dad means to say is the food is expensive so better not let it go to waste, Sam," I said.

Dad winked at me while Mom chuckled.

"Better be nice to me, Cayt," Dad warned. "School's about to start. You'll be crawling to me for help with your Algebra."

"You wouldn't withhold help from me just because of this!"

"You overestimate him," Mom said, a bit distractedly. She kept glancing in the direction of the booth beside ours.

"Hey," Dad groaned, lightly bumping his shoulder sideways onto Mom's. "You're supposed to be on my side."

Teasing, I stuck my tongue out at Dad in between guffaws. Just then, Sam raised her bowl up to her chin, chopsticks in her right hand as she posed for the camera.

"I can do it!"

But her left hand, too small for the heavy bowl, lost her grip on it so that the bowl slipped to the floor and, with a loud crash, shattered into pieces, sending precious white rice and bits of grilled chicken flying everywhere. I instinctively looked around and noticed the girl with the short blue hair straining her neck to get a glimpse of us, while the baby in the next booth started crying and his mother immediately began cooing to calm him down.

"Yikes!" I shook my head while Dad slid out of the bench, stooping to help the waitress who had hurried to our table to pick up the shards of stoneware. But Mom, to my surprise, yanked Sam out of her seat and started spanking her repeatedly on the buttocks.

"Bad girl! You are naughty and hard-headed!" Mom spat as she walloped my sister using the flat of her palms.

One, two, *three!*

Four, five, *six!*

Seven, eight, *nine!*

Ten, eleven, *twelve!*

The steady staccato of Mom's loud, sharp smacks was punctuated only by Sam's howling.

I watched, helpless, as my sister struggled without success to free herself from Mom. Stop making things worse for yourself, Sam! I willed for her to hear my thoughts.

Mom's knuckles turned white as she tightened her grip on the back of my sister's dress. "Did we not *tell* you to be careful?" she growled before raising her arm to strike at Sam again.

For a moment, Dad and I were transfixed by the sight in front of us. Then Dad snapped out of the trance and sprang into action, pulling Sam away from my mom. He hugged my sister tightly and rubbed her back to soothe her, though she wouldn't stop crying. Beside us, I could hear the baby wailing too.

I sunk low into my seat as Mom stood motionless by our table, glowering at Sam and Dad. Her face was a bright shade of red and so, I noticed, was the palm of her right hand.

Then I saw it: all the eyes in the restaurant were on us. The room was still for a few moments before slowly buzzing to life with hushed whispers. It was like Cauayan all over again.

"I think she's _ _ _ _ _."

It was as if hearing that word had awakened something in me.

"Dad," I said, rising from my seat.

"Hmm?" he answered, looking up but still holding on to Sam.

"Should I get the bill now?"

Dad looked up and looked around. "I'll do it. Here, take Sam."

I pulled a wheezing Sam gently towards me while Dad placed his hands on Mom's shoulders and coaxed her to sit down. She did, but started muttering things underneath her breath.

Dad ran to the cashier and paid there instead. Then he hurried us out of the restaurant, his arm around Mom's shoulder while Sam and I followed at a safe distance behind them.

At home, I watched from our bathroom as Dad tucked Sam into bed, her eyes still red and swollen from crying.

"Mommy doesn't love me anymore, does she Daddy?" Sam whispered.

"Shh, she does, she does," Dad murmured. "She does," he repeated even when Sam had already closed her eyes, as if he were speaking to himself. He mussed up my hair before he disappeared down the stairs, his footsteps slow and heavy.

I climbed into bed a few minutes later. But I couldn't sleep. I picked up my phone and scrolled through my old friends' posts, desperate for a distraction. A fancy kid from my former school had posted a gazillion throwback photos from her summer in Turkey, a hundred hot air balloons dotting the skies behind her. Another had posted a photo from her fourteenth birthday. She had a really nice cake with light pink frosting and rainbow sprinkles. According to the caption, her mom, a well-known caterer back in Cauayan, had made it herself.

Their lives were all so happy. Extraordinary, even, while I couldn't even get normal, couldn't go to a mall without fear of being publicly humiliated or, worse, seeing another side of my mother I wish didn't exist.

I tapped on my album and scrutinized the photos and videos I had taken at the restaurant earlier, looking for a sign that Mom had an outburst coming. Maybe a frown, a furrow of a brow. But there was none. Finally, I got to the last one, my accidental recording of the beginning of Mom's episode. It was about as scary and as shaky as *The Blair Witch Project.*

I tossed my phone away as quick as I could, but the image of Mom unleashing her fury on Sam had already been seared onto my brain. Right next to it was another image: three dozen people in the restaurant simply looking on—and not one person bothering to ask if they could be of any help.

Then again, how could other people help where one's _ _ _ _ _ was involved?

I don't think Mom was ever going to be herself again.

COLLISIONS

I was jolted awake by the sound of Dad shouting from downstairs, a note of panic and urgency in his voice. Was there a fire? A foreign invasion? A new strain of the virus that actually turned everyone *into* the walking dead?

I grabbed my phone and the screen automatically lit up. When I saw the time, I began to hope that zombies had come to take me instead.

It was already ten minutes past seven. And I was going to be late for my first day in school. Shoot!

I looked down at the pullout to my left and was surprised to find that Sam was still there too. Double shoot. Why did Mom and Dad let us sleep in?

"Cayt! Sam! Are you girls ready yet?" came Dad's voice again.

"I JUST WOKE UP!" I shouted frantically while hurriedly shaking my sister awake.

"Sam, run to Mom. We're late." Sam's face crumpled up in worry at that last word and she scrambled downstairs and out of sight.

Of all the days to sleep through my alarm! I didn't need this on top of yesterday's dinner disaster. Was there no end to my bad luck?

I bolted for the bathroom, a steady stream of curse words gushing forth from my mouth like water from a broken dam. I stripped off my oversized *Shaun of the Dead* T-shirt before climbing into the shower and unceremoniously squirting a dollop of shampoo onto my hair. I grabbed a bar of soap and hurriedly ran it over my arms and pits, then between my thighs. I turned on the water again and rinsed my hair and body, not bothering to double check if there was any shampoo or soap residue left.

So much for making a good impression on my classmates. But it was either that or a tardy mark on my class record on the first day of school.

I jumped out of the shower and grabbed a towel to dry my hair. I walked out of the bathroom, not bothering to cover my body, and was surprised to see a half-asleep Sam still in her jammies, sitting on the floor in the middle of our room. She didn't look at all like she was ready for school.

"Sam! Why aren't you ready?"

"Dad said Mommy isn't feeling well. He said you'll take care of me."

"Why can't he do it?!" I said, nearly pulling out all my hair with the towel.

"He went to buy Mommy's headache medicine." Sam looked like she was about to cry. To be honest, I felt like crying too. Instead, I forced myself to do what any older sister in the same situation would.

"Alright, take off your clothes now and get in the shower quick!" I said, trying to keep the situation—and my emotions—under control. "You can do it yourself, big girl."

While Sam was in the bathroom, I hurried to get her a light blue school dress from the closet. I laid it down haphazardly on the bed, along with a pair of frilly white socks and matching underwear. I raised my voice as I threw on the Lorenzo-prescribed knee-length navy skirt and white blouse that buttoned at the back.

"Sam, hurry up!" I shouted as I clipped on the large navy bow to the front of my blouse.

Soon after I had zipped and buttoned myself into my uniform, Sam marched out of the bathroom, her wavy black hair dripping water wherever she went. I ran to Sam and rubbed my towel all over her tiny frame. Even as she was just stepping into her undies, I was already pulling down the dress over her head.

Then I grabbed our schoolbags before we scurried down the spiral stairs.

When we reached the landing, Dad was just on his way out of the master bedroom. I looked at him, a question on my face.

"Mom's gonna be okay," Dad answered, pinching the bridge of his nose the way he did whenever he was particularly troubled. "She's just a bit sad that she won't have you girls all to herself today."

Yeah, she's so attached to us, I thought as I replayed last night's fiasco in my head.

In the background, the words and music of *Up to the Mountain* tumbled out from my parents' bedroom. How many times had I heard her put on this song in the past year? I could mark the exhaustion and weariness in the singer's voice as the track played out. Of course, it wasn't exactly the upbeat song I would've chosen to go with my first day in junior high. But it did have that soldiering-on-despite-hardships kind of message, which I could really use right now.

"Who's gonna make my lunch?" Sam quipped as we strapped on our face masks over our mouths.

I bit my lip. I knew I should've packed our lunches last night after ironing Sam's and my uniforms, seeing as Mom didn't have the pep to do it. But once Sam had stopped sniffling and had fallen asleep completely, I really felt like rewatching *Warm Bodies*. It was just one of those moments when I needed a pick-me-up to remind me that even zombies could become human again. In hindsight, staying up late before the first day of school was not the brightest idea.

Felt right at the time, though.

"Your lunch is in my wallet, sweet pea," Dad told Sam as he took out a few bills from his wallet and divided it between the two of us. You know it's an emergency when Dad doesn't hesitate to bring out cash. He didn't even seem to notice that he gave us twice more than what he used to give us back when we last attended school in person.

"Yay!" Sam cheered. My sister seemed to be recovering pretty well from last night, though I did notice her massaging her butt a couple of times while she was getting dressed earlier.

"Dad, time!" I reminded him as I made a beeline for the front door.

"Oh right, yes."

We ran out the house. Dad started the engine while I steered Sam outside, taking one last glance in the direction of my parents' bedroom before I locked the front door behind me. As we piled into our car, I felt a twinge of guilt for rushing Dad and wondered if I was being inconsiderate towards my parents. Of course I cared about Mom and didn't want to add unnecessary stress on my dad, but I was in a tight spot too. If Dad said that Mom was going to be alright, then this junior high freshman was free to focus on the more urgent matter at hand—my future.

I was running like my life depended on it, panting underneath my cloth face mask. In the corridor leading to the seventh grade classrooms, the closing chords of our national anthem grew louder with each yard that I gained. I was so close. I skidded to turn at the corner where I knew my classroom would be.

As I made the turn, I collided with someone, my nose squarely hitting her muscular shoulder. I stepped backward and found myself facing a tall, middle-aged woman with steely eyes behind small, square glasses, and reddish brown hair stretched in a tight bun. I couldn't see the rest of her face but imagined that, underneath her navy blue mask, she had thin lips that would disappear with the slightest attempt to smile and nostrils that flared angrily as she looked down at me.

I gulped and tried to avoid her gaze, catching a glimpse of the open classroom door through which some students were curiously looking on.

The teacher took me aside.

"Let's hear it," she said. "Why are you late?"

"Oh, I uh…" I stammered. This woman did not look like the sort of teacher who'd accept any excuse for tardiness, even if your mom had had a public breakdown the night before, resulting in you staying up until one in the morning in an attempt to forget what had happened and thereby causing you to wake up late and arrive at school two and a half minutes after the flag ceremony had ended. Nope. Not a chance.

And even if she were that type, I really didn't feel like divulging all of that to anybody. Telling people about Mom almost always resulted in either of two things: they either ran away from you like they could catch the plague, or they treated you like a charity case. If they believed you, most adults took the latter approach. And it was way worse with teachers because sometimes they couldn't help but give you special treatment (probably 'coz they think that's being kind) and pretty soon a bunch of kids will be making faces or using cat or dog emojis whenever you get called on during online class.

"Sorry, Ma'am. My mom isn't feeling well, so I had to take care of my sister before I could get here," I said instead. It was technically true.

"Mmm hmm," the teacher responded, which was grown up code for "yeah, right." She raised her eyebrow as she spoke. "What's your name?"

"Cayt, Ma'am," I stuttered.

"Your *full* name?"

"Cayt Valerie Vergara," I completed, mentally slapping myself on the forehead.

"Miss Vergara. Ah," the teacher said, a look of recognition dawning upon her face. "From the regional program?"

Out of the corner of my eye, I spotted a girl pop up from the same hallway I had come from, tiptoeing her way towards the classroom. She had ultra short hair and skin even darker than mine, like she had been born with it and not because she'd spent her childhood days running around rice paddies because her parents refused to give her a phone until she was ten years old like any other normal parent would. There was a mischievous glint in her eyes as she looked at me, an index finger pressed over the tie-dyed mask that covered her lips.

The sight nearly made me choke. "Ye—! Yes, Ma'am," I answered.

"I'm Mrs. Castro, the school administrator. Well," the teacher said as she puffed up her chest. "I can't believe one of our honor students is late! I would've thought someone like you would be especially excited to be going to school again. Tut tut!

Academic excellence is just half of what you need to maintain your place here, Miss Vergara. Character, discipline, respect for authority..."

I nodded, trying hard not to betray my panic that, behind Mrs. Castro, this girl was practically crawling on the floor, just a few yards away from the classroom door. I tried to keep my expression straight.

"Carry on, then," Mrs. Castro finally said as she made to turn around. The last thing I remembered was seeing the look of horror on the girl's face. Without thinking, I sprang into action and draped my arms over the school administrator, hugging her tightly.

"Why—Miss Vergara!"

"I'm so sorry, Ma'am!"

"Uhm, well. It's okay," Mrs. Castro said. I felt her fidget uncomfortably and start to pull away.

If she wasn't the type who liked being hugged by strangers then, she was probably mortified that I was so close and breathing on her. But the girl hadn't made it inside the classroom yet! I held on to Mrs. Castro even tighter and let the words pour out. I didn't have time to make anything up.

"It's just that things have been very difficult at home the past year," I found myself admitting. "But I really, really want to do well here. I want a clean leaf, no, a new slate! What I mean is I just… want my family to be happy again."

"There, there. Don't cry," Mrs. Castro patted me on the head as she uttered a familiar line. How many teachers or relatives had told me not to cry over my situation, as if crying could make it worse? Mrs. Castro gave my shoulders a squeeze before pulling away. She fished out a floral handkerchief from her pocket and handed it to me.

"This is clean, don't worry," she said as I took the handkerchief from her and wiped my eyes, surprised to find that they were damp.

Mrs. Castro gestured towards the classroom door. The girl was nowhere in sight.

"I'll just give you a warning this time," Mrs. Castro said, her gaze softening ever so slightly. She turned to go but paused mid-step. "Do still try to practice safe distancing, okay? Just a precaution."

I nodded and watched Mrs. Castro walk away before taking a deep breath and entering the classroom. The teacher asked for my name and had me look for a seat before he proceeded to discussing the syllabus for Social Studies.

I found an empty chair at the back and took a notebook and pen from my bag, trying not to make a sound as I blew my nose with Mrs. Castro's handkerchief. When I finally looked up, I saw the girl with the pixie haircut, seated a few chairs to the front, craning her neck towards me. A twinkle of mischief still in her eyes, she flashed her notebook toward me. She had scribbled "thank you" and a dozen stars on the page using purple highlighter.

For the first time all morning, I smiled.

The rest of the day went as well as could be expected. It felt good to be in school and surrounded by other kids my age, even though classes were low-key boring so far. Most of our teachers began by taking the roll and, as expected, mispronouncing my and some of my other classmates' names along the way. After that, more than a few of our teachers went over the syllabus with us and even dove into lectures right away, which made me regret not opening my schoolbooks during the summer. But between the move, rewatching Swarog's films, and Mom's _ _ _ _ _, I just didn't have the time.

Our homeroom adviser, Mrs. Aguirre, was the first to break the monotony of the day. The moment she walked in, she squealed in delight at the sight of one of our classmates' notebooks, which was covered in stickers of this anime that they were apparently both huge fans of. Mrs. Aguirre went on to check the attendance, either asking each student a question or giving them a compliment. When she got to my name, she called me "Kate" and asked if she pronounced it correctly, which I found unusual. Most teachers just assumed they were right.

"It's like 'kite,' but spelled differently," I explained.

"*Kite*?" she repeated, hesitating. I nodded to let her know she had gotten it right.

"Cayt! Awesome. So tell me, Cayt, have you danced in any hurricanes lately?"

"Huh?" I said. Now it was my turn to hesitate.

"James Bond! Anyone? Oh, come on!" Mrs. Aguirre stood up, red-faced and laughing. "This is how *tita* I am. Are none of you fans of the franchise?"

We all looked around at each other but nobody raised their hands.

"Well, I bet your parents are. Okay, quick lesson."

The class groaned.

"Don't worry, this'll be good. And short." Mrs. Aguirre started writing on the board.

"Once upon a time, in the year 2015, the gorgeous Daniel Craig reprised his role as James Bond in the movie, *Spectre*. Even if you just watch the trailer, you'll catch this line: 'You're a kite dancing in a hurricane, Mr. Bond.'" She said the last bit in what I assume was supposed to be a British accent. Then

Mrs. Aguirre turned around to reveal that she had drawn a kite inside what looked like a ball of blue cotton candy.

"What could this metaphor mean? Cayt?" she said carefully as she turned to me.

Wow, way to single me out.

"Uhm," I began, suddenly becoming conscious of the fact that there were twenty students around me and they would all hear what I would say next. There was no red LEAVE MEETING button to help me escape the situation.

"Well, it's an action film so, uhm, that he was gonna be in trouble?"

A few seats to my left, I heard somebody shout, "He's in deep shit!"

I laughed nervously, as did my other classmates.

"Excuse your French, Franz," Mrs. Aguirre said, unfazed. "But that's right, you're both right. Bond is in way over his head."

"See, what chance does a kite have against a hurricane or typhoon, right? Can you imagine it in the middle of all the flying roofs and cows and things?"

I pictured a kite being shredded into pieces by violent winds.

Mrs. Aguirre continued to prod us. "But isn't it weird that they used the word *dance*? Dancing is so graceful and skillful. Intentional. So maybe… Maybe Bond *was* in way over his head.

But he wasn't just gonna let the winds carry him wherever. Instead, he danced his way through that hurricane like a sexy beast."

"Spoiler alert!" The girl with the pixie haircut pretended to whisper to the girl next to her.

We all laughed.

"Oops! Sorry, Jorgia," Mrs. Aguirre said, playing along. Then she continued.

"But here's another spoiler for you: I'm not gonna sugarcoat. There are gonna be some tough hurricanes ahead. And I mean state of calamity. The whole world is only just recovering from a global health crisis. Our education systems are still trying to figure out this whole back-to-school thing, which basically means nothing is really certain. On top of all that, look at those textbooks! If you think it'll be hard to fit them into your lockers, try cramming them into your heads. But! But. We *can* all learn and *choose* to dance."

Mrs. Aguirre did a little dance from the new BTS music video, which had us cheering for more. But she refused and had us settle down instead so she could resume the roll again. As she took her seat, I thought I saw her wink in my direction.

"Alright, who's next?"

After our long roll call, Mrs. Aguirre handed out little brown bags to us. Inside each bag was an eraser, a pack of those tiny biscuits with rainbow-colored meringue on top, a stick of gum, and a heart-shaped sticker with different variations of her goofy face on it. She said that each of them meant something that she hoped we'd figure out and practice throughout the year. Or, at the very least, she hoped we'd wait until after school to eat the Iced Gems.

After homeroom, Mrs. Aguirre hurried out of the classroom to make way for our next teacher, who had been standing outside the door for several minutes already. As soon as he entered our room, our Math teacher, Sir Li, playfully reminded us to stow away our biscuits lest they make their way into his mouth. He asked us to introduce ourselves by prefixing our names with our dream jobs. Then he proceeded to discussing the syllabus and year-end project with us, once in a while going off-script to give us examples of how we'd need math in our future careers as engineers or social entrepreneurs or content creators and everything in between. By the time the bell rang for lunch, I had the feeling that learning math from him might actually be nice.

As soon as Sir Li left the classroom, most of my classmates jumped up from their seats as if they had been on the receiving end of an electric shock. Chairs scraped across the floor as boys and girls scrambled over to their friends, more than a handful casually taking out their contraband phones. I took my time stowing away my notebook and syllabus, pretending not to notice how most of my classmates had already emptied out of the room towards the direction of the cafeteria and canteen.

I didn't have a problem at recess earlier because twenty minutes was barely enough time for me to buy food. But now I had an entire hour. And I had run out of things to stow in my bag. Unless I was planning to disassemble my chair and stuff it in there too, I no longer had a reason to stay in the room.

I looked up and noticed that the boy who sat to my right was unstacking a metal lunch box on his desk. He saw me looking at him.

"Let's eat," he said in a rich, deep voice that I couldn't quite reconcile with the few blonde streaks peaking out from his black hair.

"Oh, no, it's okay. But thank you! Architect Law, right?"

I wanted to slap my forehead the moment I said it. I might as well be Dork Cayt.

The boy chuckled. "Or just 'Law,'" he said as he opened his lunchbox to reveal one tin stuffed with black rice and another with a light-colored pork stew. The smell of tamarind was unmistakeable and automatically made me smile, but I was surprised to see Law grimace instead.

"It's been so long since we went to school that I think my mom has forgotten how much I hate it when she packs me soups for lunch. I don't like eating them cold."

"Are you kidding me? *Sinigang* is *sinigang,* whether it's hot or not," I found myself defending his lunch. I was rarely passionate about much else apart from movies. But *sinigang* was one of the exceptions. I loved *sinigang.* And no one in the family—not even Lola or Ate Fe—could make it as well as my Mom used to.

"You want it?" he asked.

"But what about you?"

Law shrugged.

"I know," I said, pressing the tips of my fingers together the way I did whenever I felt I was on to a brilliant idea. "I'll buy a hot lunch and come back here so we can trade!"

I practically tumbled out of the row of chairs and ran out of our classroom in the direction of the cafeteria. As soon as I got there and opened the door, my ears were greeted by the cafeteria din. I made a dash for the lunch line and grabbed the hottest dish available. As I walked away from the cashier, I heard it: the unmistakable sound of my name being called (and pronounced correctly) in front of the entire crowd.

"Cayt!"

I turned around to see Jorgia, the girl with the pixie haircut, waving from one of the tables. She gestured for me to come over so I did.

"Thanks again for saving my ass back there," Jorgia said when I reached their table. Beside her were our classmates, Alex and Hallie, sipping juice and munching on their fries as if they were in a fancy restaurant.

"It's chill," I said. I turned to walk away, but then I heard one of them say my name.

"*Cayt*. What is that short for?"

"Nothing," I said. "It's C-A-Y-T though. I think that's how the nurse spelled it and it just stuck."

"Weird," Alex commented.

"Well, my Jorgia's spelled with a *J-O* so I can't talk," Jorgia said, facing them. Hallie and Alex laughed and started talking about other people they knew with weirdly-spelled names. I started to move away for the second time.

"Cayt, wait!"

I turned around when Jorgia called my name again.

"At Li's class, you said you wanted to be a filmmaker, right?" Jorgia asked.

"Uh yeah. Just a dream, really."

"No, that's cool! My parents are in the biz. They actually own, well, partly own, a micro-cinema. Do you wanna come with sometime?" Jorgia asked, pulling out the empty chair next to her. I think that meant I could sit there. "They just upgraded the ventilation."

Jorgia and I started talking about films and stuff, like how *the* Harriette Swarog herself had gone to Lorenzo before apprenticing on film sets, how Jorgia liked to experiment on scoring random videos for her TikTok, or how I had been making my own YouTube shorts for almost a year now. Before I knew it, we had devoured all of Alex's fries and Law's pork chops.

Oh no. Law's pork chops!

I stood up abruptly, sending my empty metal tray clanging across the table. It hit Alex's cup so that juice spilled onto the table in front of her. She looked absolutely horrified but I was pretty sure that I was more mortified by it all.

"I am so sorry!" I nearly cried as we all gathered to check on Alex.

"It doesn't look like you got anything on her," Jorgia said as she studied the front of Alex's blouse.

"Yeah well I'm wearing the blouse and it's friggin' wet," Alex said, her voice rising dangerously. Alex stormed towards the nearby bathrooms, followed closely by Hallie. Jorgia waved them off nonchalantly.

"Don't worry. Alex gets triggered by everything. I think she's channeling Blair Waldorf," she said. "Wanna come with to the bathrooms?"

"No, *sorryneedtohurryback*," I blurted out, remembering Law. I sprinted towards our classroom, barely registering that Jorgia shouted "later" after me.

By the time I got back to the room, some of my other classmates had also returned. I approached Law, who was packing up his canteen. I took my seat next to his and, when he looked at me, gave him my best sad puppy dog eyes.

"I'm really sorry, Law. Got held up by some girls."

"S'fine. Cold *sinigang's* still *sinigang*, right?" Law shrugged and gave me a weak smile before replacing the mask over his mouth.

Mom, back when she still paid attention to things, used to bribe me with the promise of tickets to the movies, just so I would smile for pictures during family reunions. Smiles, she said, told so much about a person, and not just whether they brushed their teeth thrice a day or drank way too much soda (or *Coks*, as my Lola would say). I've seen my fair share of them to know that this was true. There were sincere ones and mechanical ones, sad ones and even nervous ones. Over the last year, I've also become familiar with the smiles nobody wants to see—like those that took joy in embarrassing my Mom.

I knew from the way that Law's eyes refused to crinkle that his wasn't a real smile at all.

"To be honest, the pork chop wasn't that good anyway," was all I managed to say. But before Law could even respond (though I wasn't sure if he was going to since he hadn't looked up from his blank notebook), our Science teacher had arrived.

Throughout the day, I kept sneaking sideward glances at Law but he seemed really focused on our lectures. Then, as soon as the bell rang for dismissal, he scurried out of the room without a word.

I felt horrible. I knew all too well what it was like to have a classmate, even a friend, forget all about you or cast you aside. If only I could tell Law that I didn't mean to make him wait for nothing. If only I could just tell him how much I had missed talking to someone whom I shared the same obsessions with. How my Mom and I used to do that all the time but that things had changed so drastically the past year that it hurt to even just think about it.

But how could I possibly say those things without coming off like a selfish jerk or total weirdo or both?

I was still feeling glum about how the day had ended when Jorgia yelled a quick "see ya" to me on her way out. I waved and said "bye" back then walked to the back of the room, where I began shoving my books into my locker. As I struggled to fit them all in, I heard Mrs. Aguirre's voice in my head encouraging me to dance in this first of many hurricanes.

ALMOST PARADISO

It was the first weekend after school began and there was news of a storm approaching. Inside our apartment, though, it looked like a Signal 3 typhoon had already swept past our living room.

When we first arrived at Elvira, there were half a dozen boxes piled on top of each other right smack in the center of the living room. Dad, in yet another showcase of stinginess, had apparently requested the landlady not to dispose of the previous tenant's belongings, in case he could find some use in them. Since we only had a couple of weeks to settle in and prepare for school, we had simply pushed the boxes to the side and tried not to look at them whenever we passed by. But now that we had finally convinced Dad to place an order for a sofa, the boxes had to go.

Dad and I were sitting cross-legged on the floor, surrounded by all sorts of junk, which we were sorting into four piles: KEEP, SELL, DONATE, and TOSS. We had been at it since Friday night but there seemed to be no end to it. Probably because Dad kept taking the things that I had previously organized and moving them to a different pile.

"Seriously? You move everything into KEEP!"

"Honey, this is in good condition," Dad said, holding up a bronze sculpture of a naked Grecian woman. "We could use it as decoration. All it needs is a bit of professional work, maybe a paint job…"

"Ha! You? Hire a pro?"

"I'm a professional—"

"—Accountant. Not an interior designer." I wondered if this was Dad being a cheapskate or if he honestly believed that inheriting yellowing issues of Architectural Digest printed two decades ago made him an expert on the subject. Ilocanos really shouldn't be allowed to become accountants, in my opinion, because both groups are stingy enough as it is. When put together, it was a lethal combination.

"You wait and see," Dad said, his eyes twinkling. I shook my head and laughed as I went back to sorting. Some people were beyond help.

"Oh wow!"

I looked up from the handful of CDs I was dumping into DONATE, expecting to see another piece of crap in Dad's hands. But he was holding up some sort of analog vintage video camera that actually looked interesting.

"A Super 8," Dad explained as he examined the battery compartment. "Doesn't look like it still works though. Completely rusted. Too bad. You know your Mom had one as a teen?"

"Really?" I asked, trying to imagine Mom as a kid my age.

Dad was about to throw the camera into the TOSS pile but I snatched it before it could join the ugly teddy bears and books with chewed-off pages. He raised an eyebrow.

"If you're keeping that statue, I'm taking this," I said, holding the Super 8 out of Dad's reach.

"To each, her own," Dad said, laughing, and I couldn't help but join in. I guess I had some Ilocano in me, too.

Just then, *Run Rabbit Run*, which I had personally selected as a ring tone for Dad after I saw Get Out, started playing. He hoisted himself up and grabbed his phone from the coffee table. With his free hand he pointed an index finger at me. "Get back to work."

"You are a mean old slave driver," I said, making a face at Dad. The song stopped playing as he answered the phone. "*Apay*?"

With Dad preoccupied, I snuck out of the living room, Super 8 in hand, and went up the spiral stairs to Sam's and my bedroom.

To be honest, nothing could be farther from the truth. Before Mom started "letting go of herself," as Lola would say, Dad had always been the lenient one. But since then… well, Dad really rose to the occasion. He was still lenient but he became more present for me and Sam, and not just for the fun stuff either. In the last year, Dad pretty much had to be the public face of our parents. He was the one who helped us with our school modules and projects, took us to church on Sundays (I wouldn't have minded if we had skipped that), and hung out with us on an almost daily basis—all while running his small accounting business and helping Lola manage the farm. I have a newfound respect for Dad. He's semi-cool. Operative word: *semi*. There was still no explaining his unhealthy preference for buddy comedies or his Spotify playlist of nonsensical novelty songs. Mom was the one I could go to if I wanted to talk about film and art and stuff. Or just to talk, period.

Operative word: *was*.

The Mom I had now was so different from the Mom I had looked up to. She didn't cook for us or help us with our homework or ask us how our day went anymore. She no longer played dress-up with Sam or binged on movies with me or nagged Dad about work. She had turned into a completely different person. A _ _ _ _ _ woman, some said.

When I got to our room, I wiped off the dust from the Super 8 using the hem of my shirt before placing it on my bedside table.

I paused for a moment to admire it but then felt a twinge of sadness that such an extraordinary object now seemed broken beyond repair.

I heard Dad's voice calling me and went back downstairs to finish up the sorting with him.

With the previous tenants' junk donated to a local parish and some sent to Cauayan (for "storage," if Dad was to be believed), Dad figured we all deserved a treat. And I knew exactly what I wanted. Over lunch, I decided to build up my case for why we should watch *Tapang*, which was Harriette Swarog's new film about this girl who rebels against authorities and saves her shanty town from a mysterious plague that turns everyone into zombies.

"It's actually not just a zombie film though. It's also supposed to be… educational."

Dad snorted at the mention of the word *educational*. Parents. They always thought the worst of you.

"And I'm pretty sure you can watch too, Sam!" I said, bits of fried chicken flying out of my mouth. "Oops, sorry. Anyway, it's only PG-13."

"We can all watch together then," Dad said as he inched his and Sam's plates away from me.

"Yes!" I pumped my fists in the air and turned to Sam, ready to give her a high five. But my sister didn't catch on. She just sat quietly, eating her chicken and rice without looking up from her plate.

"What's up with you?" I asked, peering into Sam's face.

Sam shrugged. Her voice was barely audible when she spoke. "I don't wanna go out."

"You're kidding, right? " Back in Cauayan, Sam never missed a chance to tag along whenever our grandmother was on her way to the market or Dad was heading to the farm because it meant coming home with a bag of candy or an ice cream cone. Even when we stopped attending classes face-to-face, we still went out at least once a week. It was unlike her to turn down an opportunity to go out and ask my parents for a treat.

I noticed Sam nervously throw a glance at Mom, who was picking at her food and completely ignoring us.

"Is there anything else you'd like to do instead, sweet pea?" Dad asked, placing a hand on Sam's back.

I watched as Sam shook her head, her hands twisting at her lap.

My face fell. There goes my chance to see a Swarog film on the big screen.

Dad must have noticed my disappointment though because he placed a hand on my shoulder too. It was a few seconds before any of us said or did anything. Then Dad broke the silence.

"I've got it!" Dad said, clapping his hands together in excitement. "Cayt, how about you watch the movie—let's be honest, you're the only one who would've enjoyed that anyway—and the rest of us just drop you off and pick you back up. And on the way, we can get some of that Korean ice cream Sam keeps telling me about, eh?"

I couldn't help but hug Dad. "You're a genius!" I said.

"And don't you forget it. But Cayt, this isn't Cauayan," Dad warned as he extricated himself from my arms. "If we're doing this, you can't wander off somewhere. And you have to be careful. The virus isn't completely gone yet."

"I know, I know," I answered. "I'll be totally responsible. I'll glue my mask on."

"You better." Then Dad squatted so he was now face-to-face with Sam. "Now, who's ready for some Korean ice cream?"

"It's called 'bingsu,' Dad," Sam said, finally smiling.

"Alright! Movie for Cayt, bingsu for Sam."

I held my hand up again toward Sam. This time around, we high-fived and playfully slapped each other's cheeks with the backs of our hands—our secret sister handshake.

An hour later, I was walking up the steps leading to Cinema Paradiso, one of the remaining micro-cinemas in Metro Manila that didn't permanently shut down because of the pandemic. While bigger was better in my hometown, I guess people in the big city were looking for small and quiet places. Go figure. For me, though, it wasn't so much the size or the location of the theater that mattered. One thing I had been really looking forward to doing here (aside from walking the streets and school hallways in peace) was going to see all the good movies that they never showed at our lone shopping mall in Cauayan.

Going to the movies had been my and Mom's thing ever since she first brought me to the cinema to watch *Zootopia*. We would watch everything from animated films and local rom-coms to biopics, action movies, and my favorite zombie comedies. It drove Dad nuts because, well, money. I think he secretly rejoiced when cinemas closed for two years because of the pandemic. Some time before that happened, though, Mom had snuck me into my first R-13 film, buttering up the girl who was checking tickets so she'd let me in even if I was only ten. I could still remember sitting in the middle of a cinema that was not even half full and being as much in awe of my mother as she was by the spunky women kicking ass on the silver screen.

It was one of the few good moments with Mom that I had no trouble recalling. I'm sure there are others but, the more that time passed, the harder it was becoming for me to remember them. It was like trying to hold on to water—my fond memories of her were trickling between my fingers and in danger of slipping away completely. Watching movies, even attempting to make my own, was my way of holding on.

When I stepped inside Cinema Paradiso, I was surprised to see an old-fashioned ticket booth against the rest of the minimalist interiors. And it wasn't only for display too, but there was an actual person manning it. But when I approached the booth, the person behind the glass looked up and I was shocked to find that it was a kid. Not just any kid, too. If the dark skin and closely cropped hair didn't give it away, the name tag pinned on her cream-colored shirt did.

"Cayt! You're here!" Jorgia said, practically yelling though we were less than two feet apart. Even with her mouth covered, I could tell by the way Jorgia's head perked up and her eyes turned at the corners that she was beaming at me. When was the last time someone looked happy to see me?

"What's with your face?" Jorgia asked.

"Nothing. There's no face," I stammered defensively.

"If you say so." Jorgia shrugged. "So, did you just come to say 'hi' or are you here to watch?"

"To watch," I repeated. "I didn't even realize this was the place you were talking about!"

"Yeah, I try not to give out too many details if I can avoid it. My parents are afraid all the teachers and parents will start passive-aggressively asking for free tickets, especially now that it's safer to go to the movies again," Jorgia explained, chuckling as she held a hand up and rubbed the pads of her fingers together as if counting paper bills. "Right so, let me guess—*Tapang* for two o'clock?"

"Yeah, here's my ticket," I said, showing the QR code I had saved on my phone when I made the reservation earlier.

"Cool parents to let you come here on your own, BTW," Jorgia said as she scanned the code.

"I guess," I said, trying not to remember the last time I went out with my family. "They'd be cooler if they actually offered to pay for it."

"No, those would be perfect parents," Jorgia said, chuckling. "The main reason *I* get to go out and come here is because mine couldn't afford to keep all their old staff from before all the lockdowns. But I'm not complaining. I'd take child labor over imprisonment any day, easy."

"Ohhh, right. The lockdowns were stricter here," I said. Back in Cauayan, we could pretty much still go anywhere except to the hospitals and schools. I guess I had at least that to be thankful for despite everything else that had happened to our family the past year. Some silver lining.

"Don't tell me you've been able to go out all this time back in your province!" Jorgia said, looking surprised.

"Well, not the *whole* time," I explained. "But after the first wave, most of the places reopened again. Except if there was a surge in the number of people getting sick, obviously."

"Ugh, so jealous!"

"Don't be," I said, snorting. "We have, like, one mall, a water sports place, and a few nice cafes. Then the rest are just your standard farms and markets and stuff. Not that interesting."

"I've never been to a farm, actually," Jorgia said. "I bet that's nice."

"Would you trade this place for a farm, then?" I asked.

"Hmmm," Jorgia answered. "Maybe. I could still do an open-air cinema."

"In Cauayan? Nobody would go," I said, laughing. "It'd be too hot!"

"Give me some time to think of marketing, will ya'?"

We both laughed.

"Oh hey, you'll wanna go inside and find your seat soon," Jorgia said.

"Right, thanks," I said, checking the time on my phone before turning to leave.

"Hold up," Jorgia said. She slid something on the counter towards me.

It was a small brown bag, the kind used to wrap fresh *pan de sal* from the bakery. I looked at her, intrigued.

"Barf bag. You might need it."

"Seriously?" I hadn't read any reviews yet but I never imagined I'd feel disgust while watching a Swarog film.

"I don't even wanna talk about it," Jorgia said as she closed her eyes and made retching sounds. "Just take it and I'll catch you after."

I took the paper bag and decided to quickly explore the other parts of Cinema Paradiso before the movie started.

Out of the corner of my eye, I saw a guy approach Jorgia in the ticket booth when I left.

"You and your barf bags," he said.

"It makes people curious! Ish. And I'm not cleaning up puke again."

"Shouldn't you be at home? Where you can study?"

"That's all I've been doing the past couple of years! No way am I gonna stay at home voluntarily," Jorgia replied.

I silently nodded in agreement as I checked out the display rack of local film merchandise by the entrance. There seemed to be a snack bar at the far end of the cinema too but it was closed, probably since eating inside the cinemas still wasn't allowed.

Just before I made my way inside the screening room, I glanced back at the ticket booth. Jorgia was staring blankly into space, obviously daydreaming, an unopened book laid out on the counter in front of her. I chuckled as I skipped towards my assigned seat.

Soon after, the opening credits rolled.

I almost puked during the first ten minutes. The film was a riot.

By the time Jorgia and I bolted through Cinema Paradiso's doors, I was still gushing about *Tapang*.

"It's so cool how it shows that blind obedience can turn people into lifeless zombies," I said. "And lead to the collapse of society."

"That! But also, how Swarog made it both scary *and* funny," Jorgia added.

"She's a genius," we said at the same time. Then we both laughed.

"I'm definitely taking some cues from her for my next project," I said. Then, after just a moment's hesitation, I proceeded to telling Jorgia the premise of my story.

"So that's why you hoarded on all those face paints from film club the other day!"

"I did *not* hoard," I said, defensive.

"Whatevs," Jorgia said, laughing. "Listen, have you thought about the music?"

There was definitely a spring in my step as Jorgia and I walked into the parking lot to wait for our rides. Dad was nowhere in sight but Jorgia's ride, a pale gold sedan, was already there. Jorgia tried to open the passenger door but it didn't budge. She rapped on the heavily tinted window at the driver's side. Nothing. I watched as Jorgia pressed her face to the window and cupped her hands around her eyes to get a closer look inside.

Jorgia jerked her thumb towards the window. "Ugh. My sister's such a heavy sleeper."

"Are you sure she's okay?" I asked. Hadn't I heard of people dying because they fell asleep in their parked cars for really long periods of time?

"Well, she could also be stoned," Jorgia said.

"Seriously?"

"I'm joking. But could be… who knows? She hasn't exactly told me anything since she got a boyfriend," Jorgia said. Her voice cracked a tiny bit as she said this. Kind of in the same way mine did whenever I had to talk about Mom. "Wish my parents would just let me bike so I didn't have to put up with her driving."

Jorgia proceeded to pounding and screaming "Ate Jacq!" at the window. I did the same but with less intensity. After I dunno how many more minutes of that, I was already thinking of calling a guard but, just then, the window rolled down to reveal the person in the driver's seat.

I froze.

"Finally!" Jorgia sighed. "Dude, can you not stay awake for ten minutes?"

"Chill, Jorg. It's either I pick you up or you're stuck at home," the person said, combing her fingers through her bright blue hair. "Who's this?" she said, looking at me.

I avoided eye contact and bent down to pretend-tie my non-existent shoelaces. I could feel my heartbeat racing.

"This is Cayt. We're in the same class at Lorenzo. She's filming a zombie short and I'm gonna do the music!" Jorgia added eagerly.

"Bore! Hurry up."

"You were the one who fell asleep!" Jorgia muttered as she climbed into the passenger seat. She had barely managed to say goodbye to me and shut the car door when the engine kicked into life and they zoomed out of the lot.

I stared at the empty space where their car used to be and found myself clutching at my chest, unable to breathe.

The girl driving that car.

The girl at the restaurant during mom's breakdown.

They both had unforgettable aquamarine hair. And they were one and the same.

I heard a loud ringing in my ears that told me plainly that disaster was fast-approaching.

GORILLA, GUERILLA

Sometimes I couldn't help but wonder why a fourteen-year-old like me should be forced to deal with the situations that I had to.

Why did it have to be *my* mom, out of all the moms, who would suddenly become this person I could no longer recognize or talk to or even be seen in public with? Why did she have to turn into someone I was afraid other people would know about? And *why*, out of all the people who could've seen Mom go berserk that night, did it have to be Jorgia's sister? The absolute last thing I wanted was for Jorgia to find out who or *what* my mother was.

Not that I knew who or what she was either.

"What am I supposed to be again?" Sam asked, cutting off my train of thought.

I nearly fell off my chair when I looked up.

Sam had sneaked up on me so that, for a split second, I actually thought I had come nose-to-nose with a tiny flesh-eating zombie.

"Oh!"

"It worked!" Sam bent over, howling, and I couldn't help but join in on her laughter. I only came to my senses when I saw that Sam's eyes were tearing up.

"Careful, Sam! Your makeup!"

It took us a few more minutes to calm down. Still with a smile on my face, I started picking up the face paint pots that had scattered all over our bedroom floor. I had knocked over the film club's special effects kit when Sam surprised me. My sister got on her knees to help.

"You got me good," I said, grinning at Sam. She beamed at me.

"So, what am I doing again?" Sam asked.

I sighed and grabbed my laptop from the bed, reminding myself to be patient when I show Sam the storyboard for the nth time. Just then, several messages popped up on my notifications.

JORGIA: if we dnt go bk 2 school nxt wk
JORGIA: imma need therapy
JORGIA: srsly

I pressed the X button and quit my messaging app for good measure.

I had been ignoring Jorgia the last couple of days. It was easy enough since the typhoon had forced Lorenzo to temporarily move our classes back online. Dad had helped Sam set up her study table in our room, while I just went back to using the same apps we had used at my old school the last few years. In between our classes and modules, I'd get Sam to work on the film with me.

Productivity was turning out to be a great way to bury confusing thoughts and emotions.

I clicked on a folder and showed the screen to Sam. We scrolled through stills of her and Dad moving boxes (which were actually empty), then pretending to clean parts of the house. Finally, we reached the most recent one, which was unscripted footage of Dad instructing a couple of men where exactly he wanted our new sofa placed.

"We've done all the normal life parts and now we're doing the first zombie sighting," I reminded her. "I'm gonna shoot Dad doing whatever, then you're gonna pass by in front of the cam super quick. Dad will be a bit creeped out but he'll shrug it off and think he's just imagining things."

"And if he's not?"

"Then we'll do another take but this time *tell* him to act creeped out," I said.

Sam was checking her reflection on my phone. "I don't get this whole gorilla film thing."

"*Guerilla*," I corrected her. "It's gonna help us get a real reaction from Dad. This is how Swarog shoots amateurs," I added. "And we both know Dad can't act."

Sam giggled.

"Ready?" I asked my sister as I mounted my phone on the hand grip.

"I gotta pee first. Last time, we took hours!" Sam said, a note of accusation in her voice.

"Fine, just go down when you're ready. And quietly!" I said as Sam disappeared into the bathroom and I stood up to head downstairs. "I'm gonna go ahead to check the lights."

I left our room and climbed down the spiral staircase. When I reached the landing, I heard Dad's voice coming from the kitchen. The door was slightly ajar. I pressed the red record button on my phone camera and snuck it past the opening, expecting to see Dad at work, phone in his ear. But he was on his feet, chopping onions, while Mom watched him, her elbows propped up on the kitchen table.

"I don't need help," Mom said, the quiver in her voice just audible.

"Anna, we can't keep denying what's plain to see."

My parents were speaking in hushed voices. My ears perked up in attention the way they did whenever they sensed they were hearing something they shouldn't.

"I can fight this on my own. You *know* I can. I just need time to forget, that's all."

I knew what this was about.

Without meaning to, my head immediately summoned memories from that day. Or emotions rather. There was excitement upon dismissal from the day's online classes and, as I ran straight to my parents' bedroom, at the thought of bingeing on episodes of *iZombie* before dinner. Surprise when I slipped outside the bathroom, and cold relief that I managed to find my footing in time. Bewilderment at seeing the puddle that had caused me to slip and hearing the gushing sound of water behind the locked bathroom door. And confusion, so much of it, as Dad banged urgently on the door while Ate Fe scurried to look for the keys.

Dad put down the knife on the chopping board and, setting it aside, pulled a chair towards him and sat beside Mom.

"It's not that we want to forget what happened. We don't. We just… need to move forward. So we can be ourselves again, love."

I sensed a pleading in Dad's voice, a grave seriousness that I felt almost embarrassed to have heard. He had only ever spoken in that tone in front of me or Sam a handful of times before, and none of them were pleasant occasions. Yet I strained my ears for more.

"I'm not yet ready."

"Then when?" Dad asked, his voice rising as he slammed a fist on the table. "*When* will you be ready, Anna?"

I didn't hear Mom answer.

"I'm sorry. I'm sorry," Dad whispered. "Please, just try to understand. We can't stay this way forever. You have to get help. *We* have to."

The kitchen was silent. I checked my screen but couldn't tell if Mom was just speaking softly or if she wasn't saying anything at all.

"For our girls, okay?"

I inched away from the kitchen door and put my phone back in my pocket.

My parents were having a disagreement again. Those had become a bit more common over the last year. I know because I kept having arguments with Mom too—about insignificant things such as my audio being too loud while I watched videos of cute dogs and babies, or leaving the door to the spare room open after I had been there to get some stuff. I often thought maybe I was having an off day and it was my little mistakes that annoyed Mom. It took me half a year to realize that maybe she was actually going through something that had nothing to do with me. There was something not quite right in the way Mom's behavior shifted rapidly, how extreme her moods could be, or how the most minute and unimportant things would suddenly cause her to throw a fit.

The silence in the kitchen was punctuated by Sam's quick footsteps on the staircase. Not wanting my little sister to see my parents that way, I decided to act fast. As soon as Sam reached the bottom step, I whisked her away from the kitchen and out through our front door.

"But I thought—? Where are we going?" Sam asked, looking puzzled.

"Test shoot," I said, looking up and down the street. Then I was struck by an idea. "Wanna see how Mrs. Suaco will react when she sees you?"

"That's wicked! Let's do it," Sam said, looking very unzombie-like the way she jumped up and down in excitement.

I suddenly imagined the rollers coming off of our landlady's gray hair and her coffee-stained dentures popping out of her mouth when she shouts in surprise at the sight of Sam.

"Let's hope she doesn't get a heart attack," I muttered under my breath as I got my phone ready. I looked at the screen and realized it was still recording. I stopped the video and adjusted the settings before following Sam to our landlady's front door.

Sam and I had a blast scaring our neighbors and then receiving their compliments on her makeup and costume. When we returned home, I made my sister wait in the living room while I located my parents. Once I was sure Mom was in their room and Dad was alone in the kitchen, Sam and I shot the scene as we had planned and it turned out as well as I could've expected.

After getting over his initial shock, Dad pelted us with the boiled peanuts he had been snacking on, probably annoyed that we had successfully pulled a prank on him. I recorded that too. I got a lot of great footage from the afternoon.

I transferred the videos to my laptop then let Sam put on *Inside Out*. Letting her use my laptop was the least I could do in exchange for her helping me out, even though she did insist that I give her gummy bears upfront for the next shoot.

"Today was fun. I like it better when school's just online," Sam said as the opening credits came on.

"You're kidding, right? Maybe you're just not used to it yet," I told Sam as I bumped my shoulder gently against hers. "Cafeteria food is a nice change from Dad's cooking. And school's *way* better when you get to hang out with your classmates in person."

Well, most of the time, I thought to myself. I still didn't know how to face Jorgia once live classes resumed.

"I'm okay if I don't get to see my classmates," Sam said, shrugging. There was something in the way my sister avoided my gaze and looked down at her hands that made me feel a bit uneasy.

"What's wrong? Are they bullying you or something?" I asked, my mind already weighing whether it would be more effective to intimidate Sam's classmates or just report them to the principal.

"No," Sam answered. "I just feel weird, that's it."

"Oh. Well, maybe you are," I teased. "You know your head is almost always tilted to one side. That's definitely not normal."

"Ha ha ha. Just gimme the chips, the movie's starting!"

"Magic word?" I asked, leaning away from Sam and holding the bag of corn chips at arm's length.

Sam dove towards me, tickling my underarms and forcing me to drop the bag so I could cover my armpits with my hands. She cried gleefully as she snatched the bag from the floor.

"You could've saved two seconds if you just said 'please.'"

Sam stuck her tongue out at me before reclining on the pillows and ripping the bag open.

While my sister watched Joy get mad at Sadness for ruining everything, I revisited dozens of bookmarked pages on my phone—articles and vlogs by therapists and mental health experts on Instagram and YouTube—about how an illness called bipolar disorder could turn normal and happy people into zombies who locked themselves up in their rooms on some days, or exploded with anger on others. And how this same illness could make my mother want to kill herself.

WE CALLED HIM MIGGY

Whatever I was expecting when my parents announced almost two years ago that Mom was gonna have a baby, it wasn't this.

When I was five and Sam was still growing inside of her, Mom could hardly stay awake to join us for dinner. But this time around, it was like she was on some kind of natural Red Bull. It wasn't advisable for pregnant people to go out much because of the virus so Mom basically had to find a way to release all her extra energy within the walls of our home in Cauayan.

She redecorated the baby corner in the living room four times in the span of six months (Sam and I had started dragging our feet by the third), experimented with a kajillion recipes that all had moringa in them (which she'd make us eat afterwards but which Sam and I would throw over the fence when Mom wasn't looking), and stayed up late each night reading about succulents (as her Pinterest account would reveal the next morning).

Mom even started meddling with Dad's and Lola's businesses, which was weird because she used to always say that creating some distance between one's spouse and in-laws was necessary for inner peace or something. On some occasions when our grandmother had too much work and not enough patience for her ideas, Mom could be seen storming out of the kitchen (and Sam and I would know to stay clear from the firing range). But despite the chaos, it was kinda amusing to watch this all go down. Like a weird and moody family circus had come to town and set up camp at our home. It was a welcome distraction from the fact that lots of people were getting sick or losing their jobs and that online classes sucked big time.

Then, after eight months, Mom gave birth to our brother.

We named him Miguel (but agreed to call him Miggy) and he was the tiniest, cutest thing ever. I wanted to carry him right away but couldn't because he had to stay in an incubator at the hospital and kids weren't allowed to visit during the pandemic. So Sam and I contented ourselves with ogling at him via video call that entire weekend he was born.

When Monday came, our parents brought Miggy home. But instead of a cooing infant, Miggy was tightly swaddled and unmoving, the skin on his tiny face pale and gray.

It was the first time I had ever seen Dad cry. Tears streamed down his face and fogged up his glasses as he kissed Miggy's forehead. Then he told Sam and me we could do the same. Miggy's skin felt soft and cool as I pressed my lips against it.

And then Dad gave Miggy back to Mom. She held him delicately, looking intently at his face as if she were trying to carve every detail into her memory. When she held Miggy up to her lips so she could kiss his forehead, his closed eyes, and his tiny nose, I was sure Mom would break down in tears.

But she didn't. Her eyes just stayed on Miggy the whole time. Eventually, Dad took him and the two of them left with the men from the funeral home who were dressed in head-to-toe protective gear. Mom's gaze remained on our front door, even as Lola and Ate Fe started talking about preparations for the funeral.

Miggy's wake was the only one I had ever been to since our grandfather died. For three days, relatives and neighbors and people I didn't know trickled into our house to pray by his little white coffin. Sam and I and a few older cousins mostly hung out by the buffet, snacking on candies and rice cakes late into the night while the grown-ups talked or prayed or played cards among themselves.

And not once during this entire time did I see Mom cry. But maybe that was because I rarely saw her, period. She mostly locked herself up in their room whenever there were more than three visitors at a time. She would join the service every night but would disappear right after the priest sprinkled holy water on Miggy's coffin, before any more old neighbors and distant relatives could slip off their face masks to talk to her about God's will or being strong or looking on the bright side.

After the funeral, when we laid Miggy next to Lolo in the family mausoleum, things slowly started returning to normal. Dad only teared up on occasion, and Lola started wearing bright-colored clothes again. Ate Fe could be heard humming once more as she cooked for my Dad's and grandma's staff. Sam and I had even resumed our petty quarrels, like when we were helping Dad and Ate Fe pack the baby's things up (Sam was whining about me ordering her around all the time so I told her to zip it and hand me a cardboard box).

But Mom stayed put in their room. Days passed and turned into weeks, a month then two, and still nothing. Until that one day.

It was a Wednesday morning. Our grandmother had already left for the farm, while Ate Fe had just started on the laundry. Sam and I were pecking on our fried bananas when Mom walked into the dining room just like that. I stared open-mouthed as she pulled up her chair and sat next to us, scooping a mountain of rice onto her plate like she hadn't eaten the entire time she was cooped up in their room. Dad—who had just poured himself a cup of coffee—accidentally spit some of it out when he saw Mom in her usual seat. Dad and I caught each other's eyes and I used mine to ask him what we should do. He seemed to understand because he held up his hand, which I took as him telling me to chill while he handled things.

"Well! Good morning!" Dad said with the energy of a clown at a birthday party.

Dad was handling it, alright. Just very poorly. I made a face at him. We weren't even the "good morning" greeting type of people!

But in spite of Dad being so obvious, Mom said "good morning" back. It was so weird. Beside me, Sam remained oblivious to the awkwardness, glued as she was to some YouTube video of toys being flattened by a machine with spikes.

"Eggs, love?" Dad tried again, dropping creepy cheeriness level down by four notches.

Better.

Mom took the plate from Dad, piling two fried eggs on hers. After a mouthful, she spoke.

"I was thinking we should do a Dirty Santa this Christmas," Mom said casually.

"What's that?" Sam piped up at the mention of Christmas.

"Oh, it's just a different way of exchanging gifts. You can steal gifts from other people, given certain rules, of course," Mom added. She had always been in charge of our celebrations.

While Mom continued to explain the rules to Sam and me, Dad looked on, as if fascinated by the sight of a woman talking to her kids. After a few minutes, Mom started hurrying us up to get ready for class.

Mom was her usual chatty shelf as she hung around with us at the bathroom, occasionally instructing Sam to clean her belly button or rub behind her ears. Dad dropped in to listen and caught my eye in the bathroom mirror while I was brushing my teeth. We were both probably wondering why Mom hadn't even mentioned Miggy at all. But I was old enough to know I shouldn't force the topic. I didn't even want to bring up the fact that she had locked herself up in their room for eight weeks.

But then, I had a little sister. And she had a mouth.

Just as she got out of the bath tub and Mom was squeezing water from her wet curls, Sam quipped, "Should we still get Miggy something for Christmas too?"

Dad froze, while my eyes bulged in Sam's direction. Was I this dense when I was her age?

But Mom knelt down beside my sister, tucked stray hair strands behind Sam's ears, and smiled at her, saying, "You could make him something, if you want to. And no one would steal it from him."

I let out a sigh of relief and dragged Sam to our bedroom and away from Mom before she could say other inconsiderate things.

Right after the day's online classes, I went downstairs to look for a snack, as was my custom. I saw Mom tending to her once-forgotten but still living collection of cacti out on the patio, Sam eagerly repotting a few bulbs beside her. When Mom saw me, she ushered Sam and me into the kitchen, where she cooked and ate egg noodles with us before shoving us back into our room to do our homework. After dinner, we huddled together in the living room, Mom and Lola and Ate Fe watching this long-running cop series on television, Dad poring over receipts, Sam on the tablet, and me on my phone. It was all pretty normal.

The exact same thing happened on Thursday too. Though it was nice, it was also a bit bewildering to have Mom present at the table again. But come Friday, the whole family had slipped back into its routine almost as easily as if the last two months had never happened.

Or so I thought.

My classes ended late that day. A typhoon would be making landfall in Cauayan so a lot of our teachers were trying to cram in as many points as they could in case the power went out and we couldn't resume classes for a while. By the time I had shut down my laptop, Sam had gotten dibs on our parents' tablet and was already halfway through some anime. As I had my own plans to binge-watch all five seasons of this old show about a female zombie detective for the rest of the weekend (or until the storm causes us to lose our internet), I headed to my parents' bedroom to watch on their television instead.

But I never made it there that night. After finding the puddle outside the locked bathroom and alerting Dad, things just happened so fast. I managed to catch a glimpse of an unconscious Mom in the tub before Dad practically locked Sam and me up in Lola's room and tasked Ate Fe to watch over us while he took Mom to the hospital. We kept bugging Ate Fe to tell us what was going on but all she said was that it wasn't her place to say anything and that Dad would be the one to explain. She kept pacing back and forth across the room as we waited for news from Dad.

The sound of the rain pounding on our roof and the wind howling at us from outside the windows was earsplitting. But from our parents and Lola, there was only silence. Ate Fe—maybe because she couldn't stand not doing anything for very long—yelled at Sam and me to come with her. We got on our feet and followed her to the kitchen so we could all make *dendelot*.

Despite our requests in the past, Ate Fe had always refused to make the sticky rice cakes anytime that wasn't Lent. We were only supposed to have it when we were abstaining from meat, she said. That she voluntarily made them now—four months earlier than usual—should've troubled me. But my devotion to *latik* pushed all horrible thoughts aside and, in no time at all, Sam and I were too busy ladling sweet caramelized coconut sauce over rice cakes to even think about where or how our parents were. Our grandmother joined in when she arrived and we forgot all about her diabetes or what a proper dinner should be like. Instead, we devoured bowlfuls of *dendelot* and staked out in the kitchen until our bellies groaned.

The next morning, I woke up beside Sam on Lola's bed, wondering why my face was half-covered in flour. It took me a minute or two to recall but, once I did, I ran out of my grandmother's bedroom and into the dining room.

Empty.

I went to the kitchen—also empty.

I already had half a mind to wake Sam up and hail a tricycle to the hospital when I heard the rumble of engines and the distinct crunch of heavy tires on gravel, which told me that a car was making its way onto our driveway.

I ran out of the house and saw that the storm had passed, though the concrete was still dark and damp from the rain. My grandmother alighted from our car first, helping Mom find her footing. They were soon assisted by Dad. I skidded up to them, ready to bombard them with a million questions.

"What happened? What's going on? Is everything okay—?"

"—Not now, Cayt," my grandmother cut me off as she took of her mask and led Mom into our house.

My face fell as I stopped following them. Was it so wrong to ask questions?

"It's alright." Mom's voice was faint and hoarse, but also firm.

"Anna," Dad said. "You should rest first."

"It's okay, Eric. Sit with me, Cayt."

Mom sat me down next to her on the couch and held my hand, while Dad and Lola looked on with bated breaths. I tried to ignore them and focused on Mom instead, looking at her expectantly. I was afraid of what I would hear. And by the looks of it, so were Dad and my grandma. But I had to know. I knew something was up. I just wanted to understand.

"Yesterday, I took too many pills," Mom started. "I went to take a bath and I… fell asleep."

"Why did you take the pills?"

"Your Mom had a headache," Lola butted in.

"Not exactly. But I wasn't feeling well," Mom said, nodding. "I just wanted a relief… from the pain I was feeling."

"But—"

"Oh, Cayt! What does it all matter?" It was my grandma again. "The important thing is your Mom's here and she knows not to make the same mistake again. Right, Anna?"

The way Mom nodded made me feel she didn't really know it the way Lola wanted her to.

"Now let's get you a nice plate of *dendelot*. The girls and I stayed up all night making them." Lola continued talking to Mom as she dragged her in the direction of the kitchen. I stayed put on the couch, feeling quite sick of the sugary stuff already.

"Cayt," Dad said as he sat next to me, his voice soft. He took a deep breath.

"How do you feel about losing Miguel?"

That was an unexpected question. I paused and gave it some thought.

"Sad, of course. But," I had started to say. Then I stopped myself because it seemed like something Sam would say, which meant it was probably silly.

"Yes? Go on, Cayt."

"I dunno. I mean I wish he was here but… it's not like we ever had him with us, right? I didn't even really get to see him before he, y'know… died."

I looked up at Dad, feeling my face grow hot the moment the words escaped my mouth. But when Dad nodded, a wave of cold relief washed over me. He held my head to his chest and kissed me on the forehead.

"I understand," Dad whispered into my ear. "But it's different for Mom. Miggy *was* with her, inside of her. That's why it's harder for her."

"That's why she took the pills… to make the pain go away?"

Dad didn't answer but continued to hold me close to him. I started to feel uncomfortable, like I couldn't breathe. Not because he was hugging me tightly but because something unthinkable was forming in my head. My heart was pounding.

I squirmed out of Dad's arms and searched his eyes for an answer. "Things were so hard that Mom wanted to… she was going to—"

"—No, of course not," Dad said before I could finish. "She made a mistake."

I stared at the far end of the room where I knew, just behind the wall, Mom was. She may have worked in film but Mom had always known her way around medications because her parents were pharmacists. She used to joke that her third word after *Mama* and *Papa* was *Amoxicillin*.

Was it possible that Mom wanted to do this?

The whole concept of suicide or depression wasn't new to me. But that's just it. It was a concept—not something that I thought would ever affect someone I knew.

Especially not Mom.

"It was a lapse in judgment. Mom loves us and wants to be with us," Dad continued, his voice cracking. He took a deep breath before speaking again. "Let's just help her and be patient with her, okay?"

I nodded, even though I didn't really know how I could be of any help.

"Cayt, I need you to keep everything between us. People outside—your friends or teachers, our neighbors—none of them need to know about what happened."

"But why?" I asked, a little confused.

"Not everybody will understand what Mom is going through. But I think… if we just act normal, if we avoid anything that'll upset Mom, it'll help her recover," Dad said as he placed a hand on my shoulder. "Do you understand, Cayt?"

I looked up at Dad, and noticed how bloodshot his eyes were, like he had either been crying or accidentally gotten soap in them. Either way, he looked tired.

I wanted to be helpful so I nodded, just as Mom did a while ago. That was good enough for Dad. He got up to follow Mom and Lola into the kitchen, but I crawled back into bed next to Sam, unsure as to what exactly I had agreed to.

It wasn't too hard to keep my promise to Dad, at least within our own family. If the grown-ups in the house hardly brought up Miguel or Mom's last pregnancy, then they most definitely didn't mention anything about Mom's more recent trip to the hospital.

Sam and I, even Dad and Ate Fe, had been used to calling each other *bagtit* when we were messing around. But now, the adults would stop mid-sentence whenever they caught themselves saying it and would suddenly be all serious. They consciously avoided using the Ilocano word for "_ _ _ _ _" and any other translation or variation thereof. Even saying regular words like *baby* and *pills* were automatically banned from the household.

And it wasn't just the words that they overreacted to. After Mom overdosed on the pills, the grownups started reading into everything that Mom did or didn't do. I'd often walk in on Lola and Ate Fe whispering about Mom in the kitchen.

Did Anna get up today? Did she eat? Maybe she ate too much? Or too little this time?

Did she talk to anyone today? What did she say?

Pretty soon, I was doing the same thing too.

Mom's reading a book. Is it a funny book or a sad one?

Mom wore black three days in a row. Is that a bad sign?

And we weren't the only ones who were paying attention.

When school reopened in the new year, Mom's absence was felt. When she stopped coming to church with us on Sundays, distant relatives or acquaintances would ask us what was the matter with her. When Dad was the one who showed up for the parent-teacher conference, my homeroom teacher asked me about it, and so did some of my friends and their parents.

At first, these didn't bother me. People seemed genuinely concerned about Mom and sorry about what happened to Miggy. Then something changed.

Just a few weeks after we were allowed back in school, news spread of Mrs. Britanico's husband and teenage daughter dying from the virus. It had caused a stir in our neighborhood because there hadn't been a severe case in months. But four days after the funeral, our sixth grade reading teacher was back at school, terrorizing students again as if she hadn't just lost her entire family.

After that, whenever my teachers or our neighbors would ask about Mom, it was kinda like they were wondering why she wasn't back to normal either. Some of them asked me point-blank why Mom was taking unusually long to recover.

Once, I made the mistake of wondering aloud in front of Lola if Mom was experiencing a mood disorder like depression. She tutted and told me that mothers can't afford to be depressed because they had to be strong for their children. Then she went on to recount how, during the Martial Law era, her husband had been forced to go into hiding for nearly a decade, leaving her to make a living and raise my dad and his older brother all on her own.

When I said the same thing to Dad and asked if we should take Mom to see a therapist, he defended that Mom hadn't been locking herself up in her room anymore and didn't seem to be a threat to herself at all. Then he reminded me to do my part and be a good girl. Not wanting to be on the receiving end of more admonitions or long-winded stories from a bygone era, I decided to just keep my theories to myself after that.

I pretty much kept everything to myself, actually.

Even if Dad hadn't made me pinky-promise not to broadcast any of the events involving Mom, I just literally *couldn't* explain to my friends what was going on with her. I couldn't explain how she could be cool and buy Sam and me treats or help us with homework on some days—then be a walking volcano, ready to erupt at the slightest provocation, on others. I *couldn't* tell them how she was doing because I didn't know either and usually just tried to figure out who she was gonna be—happy Mom or zombie Mom—on a daily basis by listening to the weight of her steps or the sound of their bedroom door closing on her way out each morning.

Maybe the only thing I could explain was how I felt: how I was beginning to feel ashamed that my mother had turned into someone unlike the other mothers, or her old self even. How she had become someone who was so difficult to be around. I knew it didn't seem at all like the type of emotions a good girl, a good daughter, would have. But I couldn't help it. Not when she insisted on ruining everything for me.

Right before finals, I made the mistake of having my classmate, Mai, over for a study session. It was the first time I had a friend come over since Mom (I think) tried to kill herself.

Of course, Mai didn't know that. Or at least, I hoped she didn't. She definitely acted like she didn't, the way she was being such a pain about me insisting we do our homework in the patio, under the scorching heat of the sun, to avoid Mom.

"Cayt, it's boiling! Can't we stay inside? You know, where there's a fan?"

I looked up from my practice sheets and glanced at my friend. Beads of sweat were dripping down her nose and the sides of her face.

"I told you n times already," I said, half sighing but also half proud of myself for using "n" in a sentence. "Open air is still best. Besides, Mom's in a prickly mood. Lately, she's been acting… weird."

Weird was one way to describe my mother, I guess.

"This is the woman who recently turned your house into a mini forest," Mai said, gesturing at the varied plants and succulents that had taken over every inch of the patio and spilled onto our driveway so that the rear end of our SUV jutted dangerously out into the street. "The same woman who wrote and illustrated a malunggay cookbook while she was pregnant last year, sent the e-book to all the parents in our batch, and even wanted to do a virtual cook-off on Zoom. She's been weird for a lot longer than lately."

I paused to consider what Mai had said.

I don't know if it was because she didn't grow up in Cauayan like most of us but Mom had always been a bit different from the other adults. She always spoke her mind about politics or religion or whatever, even if nobody else shared her opinion. She insisted on only inviting a few people over for occasions, people we actually liked, which Lola disapproved of, saying it gave our family a bad reputation among our relatives and neighbors. Mom wasn't the type to give gifts either—she almost always made stuff or took us out for quality time instead. And she never punished or ordered Sam and me around but would often explain to us what we had done wrong or ask us to make choices for ourselves.

She had been a good kind of weird. But sometime during the last year or so, her weirdness took a different turn altogether.

"What if I got you a soda, would that help?" I asked Mai, changing the subject.

"Better than nothing," Mai said, shrugging as she wiped her sweaty forehead with the back of her hand.

I snuck inside the house and tiptoed my way into the kitchen, keeping my eyes peeled for any sign of Mom. But there was only Ate Fe, her head resting on the countertop as she napped. Careful not to make a noise, I plucked a bottle of soda from the fridge and filled a cup before sprinting back to the patio.

"Now tell me how you divide fractions," I demanded, holding the cup ransom.

"All you have to do is flip one of them," Mai began as she grabbed the cup from me, sliding down her mask over her chin to take a gulp. But in half a second, she spat out and spewed soda all over our practice sheets.

"What the—?" I said, jumping out of my seat, narrowly avoiding getting sprayed in the face.

"Sarsi?! You know I can't drink regular soda."

"Oh. Sorry," I said distractedly as I attempted to blot my homework dry using the hem of my shirt. "It's technically RC. And you're not supposed to drink any type of soda, right?"

"Yeah but sugar-free makes me feel less guilty," Mai admitted sheepishly.

I chuckled as I said, "That's all we have though."

"It's fine. But take it before I get tempted!" Mai said, pushing the cup back toward me.

"Thanks but I only drink spit-free soda," I teased.

I turned to my side to survey Mom's collection of plants. Dad always said not to waste anything. Noticing the dry, light brown soil underneath a particularly large rose cactus, I dumped the cup's remaining contents over it and watched the earth darken with moisture before turning my attention again to question number twelve.

Mai and I continued reviewing, arguing loudly over our answers as we did. By item number twenty-seven, though, Mom had joined us on the patio, plastic watering can in hand. I drew a sharp breath. How would Mom act around Mai or respond to her being here? But she didn't seem to notice us as she swept past our table and made a beeline for her plants. Mai and I exchanged looks for a second before returning to our worksheets in silence.

Exhaling, I turned my attention back to the page before me. I stared at the equation, which suddenly seemed like a bunch of numbers and letters squished together at random. Shifting in my seat, I stole a glance at Mom to check if she was doing anything unusual. She seemed to be repotting a few bulbs.

Everything is fine, Cayt, I told myself. I squinted at my worksheet again and, after a few seconds, finally figured out how to start solving for Z. I started scribbling. A few minutes passed before I realized that Mom was talking to me. I looked up from my workbook.

"I was asking if you watered my plants?" Mom said, a crease forming between her brows.

It was only when she asked that question that I began to consider the possibility that I may have done something wrong.

I fidgeted nervously towards Mai, whose face was sweating buckets by now.

"Why is my plant wet?" Mom asked as she lifted the ceramic pot that held the rose cactus to her face, her brows knitting together. Then a look of recognition as she sniffed at the plant. "Is that… soda?"

"No—"

"No!"

Mai and I answered at the same time, her a bit more defensively than me. Mom shifted her gaze between us before it landed on the empty cup on the table. She took it and, in a voice both calm and sinister, asked, "What was in this?"

Neither Mai nor I had the courage to look at Mom, let alone answer.

"Cayt Valerie, what was in this?"

I sat quietly, my knees trembling at the thought of what was about to come.

"Auntie—" I heard Mai begin to say.

"IF YOU DON'T TELL ME RIGHT NOW, CAYT, I SWEAR…"

For crying out loud, speak, Cayt!

But I couldn't. And before I knew it, Mom was pulling me by the front of my shirt towards her. I closed my eyes, bracing myself for the now-familiar slap across the cheek or pinch in the groin that had recently become Mom's preferred disciplinary tactics.

"Stretch out your arms," I heard Mom say instead.

I froze. It was a punishment I hadn't been given in years. I opened my eyes to search Mom's face for a sign that she wasn't serious.

She definitely wasn't joking. But she didn't look angry either. Her lips were neither pursed nor smiling, her eyes, neither narrowed nor crinkled. It was as if she was empty of all emotion. A lifeless zombie.

"Arms out," she said, her voice flat.

I had been trying my hardest not to cry because Mai was there. But there was something too painful in the way Mom looked blankly at me, as if I was nobody to her.

"Don't make me repeat myself," my mother warned.

I hesitated. Then, slowly, I stretched my arms to my sides, palms facing the ground, to form a cross. I felt my face flush with anger and embarrassment, my tears cold as they slid down my warm cheeks.

"Now turn around."

A loud sob escaped between my lips upon hearing these last words. I didn't want to turn around. Doing so meant showing my face to the rest of the street. I regained my voice.

"No, Mom, please. I'm sorry!"

Grabbing me by my shoulders, Mom spun me around herself and pulled up my arms so I'd be forced to raise them even higher.

I hung my head as low as I could, catching sight of a few curious passers-by before I could train my eyes on the concrete floor that darkened where my tears pooled. It wasn't long before I began to feel a burning sensation on the underside of my outstretched arms. My upper limbs grew heavier and I struggled to keep them raised with each second that passed.

"One hour," Mom hissed with a final tug at my arms before storming away.

A few minutes went by. Then Mai's voice, unusually gentle and low, interrupted my sobs.

"Cayt—"

"—Go away," I whispered without looking up.

It was silent for a while.

I had stopped crying. Then there was the shuffling of paper followed by light footfall that grew softer in the distance, telling me that Mai had gone.

Finally, I was alone.

That was the last time I hung out with anyone in Cauayan. I avoided Mai and my other friends after that. Eventually, they stopped talking to or messaging me, or reacting to my Instagram stories, or asking me to hang out. But while they didn't talk to me, I suspected that they talked *about* me.

At the end of the school year, happy Mom insisted that she be the one to join me to claim my report card, probably in an effort to make up for all the times angry zombie Mom smacked or screamed at us. When we arrived, we saw that a mini stage had been set up in the classroom for picture-taking purposes. It must have been the school's way of still giving us that graduation ceremony feel.

After claiming their card, each student had a chance to pose onstage with a faux diploma. I stepped up to the platform when it was my turn, handing over my phone to Mom after carefully selecting the proper settings. But instead of taking my photo, Mom turned to the rest of the parents and students waiting in line and, without warning, began to hum a graduation march very loudly. She kept waving her hands in the air like a conductor as she tried to get the rest of them to join in.

A few did, but most of them gave her funny looks. A handful started taking videos. All eyes were trained on Mom—on us. And soon, the air was buzzing with whispers. I stepped off the stage and tugged at Mom's elbow so we could leave. On our way out, I heard somebody mutter under her breath:

"*Bagtit.*"

I looked around, trying to find where it had come from, but it was hard to tell. Even with their face masks, though, I could tell more than a few people were sniggering. Then I saw Mai, sitting next to her mom, a pained expression on her face. Our eyes met briefly. Then she looked away.

I still can't remember who had started running first. All I knew was that, one minute, Mom and I were walking down the corridor and the next, we were in the car, using the fronts of our shirts as bibs to wipe tears and snot from our faces.

On the drive home, I took out my phone and stared at old photos of me and Mai and our other friends. I had expected that things would return to how they were once Mom was back to normal. But now I was sure that neither of those things was ever gonna happen.

BETTER ON MY OWN

My heart stopped. I was nearly at the Lorenzo gate when a pale gold sedan rolled up right in front of me. I held my breath as the car door swung open, bracing myself for the dreaded sight of aquamarine hair. But it wasn't Jorgia's sister behind the wheel. Just some dad dropping off three kids.

I breathed a sigh of relief. False alarm, Cayt.

Over the weekend, I had resolved to keep to myself as I had for the better part of the last school year. The less time I spent with Jorgia or the other kids at this new school, the less chances of them finding out about Mom's _ _ _ _ _ and rejecting me for it. This was my plan for getting through the next four years of junior high unscathed. I can't be sad to lose friends if I didn't have any in the first place, right?

I thanked my lucky stars when I arrived at the classroom and saw that Jorgia wasn't there yet (which made sense because, according to her, her sister hates waking up early). I dumped my things under my desk and sprinted to the library. The other part of my plan was to stake out there every morning to avoid having to talk to any of my classmates.

The library was deserted when I got there. As expected. I wandered around the shelves in the fiction section and was surprised to find a musty copy of *Pet Sematary*. Both movie versions had me sleeping with the lights on for two full weeks. No wonder this book looked like it hadn't been picked up since it was placed on the shelf ages ago!

I grabbed the book, half expecting it to disintegrate into confetti in my bare hands. It didn't, so I started reading. I made slow progress but managed to reach page nine before the first morning bell rang. I got up from my seat and jammed the book back into the shelf before jogging back to our room.

By the time I got there, most of the students had already assembled in the hallway for the flag ceremony. Jorgia's head, with her pixie-cut hair, was hard to miss as it bobbed animatedly next to Alex's. I kept my head down and made a beeline for my place, passing by a small cluster of my classmates being told off by our first period teacher to discuss yesterday's basketball scores at recess instead. And even as I heard my name called a couple of times, I continued to engross myself in tearing off an imaginary hangnail from my index finger. Quietly, I willed for the final bell to ring while, just a few steps from me, I heard our teacher shush Jorgia.

The rest of the day could not go by any slower as I kept trying to avoid Jorgia. When the bell for recess rang, she came up to my seat near the teacher's desk but, before she could utter more than a "hey," Sir Li asked her to step outside the classroom with him. That was a relief, although I did hope Jorgia wouldn't get in trouble for that new ear piercing (we were only allowed one on each earlobe).

At lunch, she hollered at me to come join her, Alex, and Hallie at the canteen. I said I'd follow after I finished jotting down my notes but, as soon as they disappeared, I packed up my notebook and took out my lunch. Law, who had been sitting next to me the entire time, gave me a funny look as I took a bite of my sardine and lettuce sandwich.

We ate our lunches in silence. In a matter of minutes, I had finished mine while Law was only halfway through his adobo and rice. Man, I think I'm gonna need to learn to cook more stuff. Don't think Sam and I can last the whole school year on just sandwiches.

"Want some?"

Law's deep voice pierced my thoughts. Oh no. Had I been staring hungrily at his lunch the entire time?

"No, I'm good! Thank you," I said, embarrassed.

"Come on, let's share. My Mama always overpacks my lunchbox."

Before I could politely refuse, Law grabbed the lid of his lunchbox and split the remainder of his rice and braised pork with me. "Here. I have extra utensils too."

I could feel my face grow really warm. I tried to shoo Law's hand away but he wouldn't budge so I gave in. Might as well make the most out of my embarrassment, right?

"Thanks," I said sheepishly as I used Law's spare fork to dig into his lunch.

We continued to eat in silence before Law broke it. "It's a little salty."

"No, it's perfect!" (Dad always told me that free food tastes great no matter what.)

"Mama likes everything salty. Which is probably why we're all, you know…"

I looked at Law, waiting for him to finish his sentence.

"…Fat."

I coughed and covered my mouth as I choked on a bit of pork. "I can't believe you called your family *fat*. When you're really just… large-bodied?" I insisted.

"That's a load of crap. I am fat."

"Wow," I said, stifling a laugh. "You seem so cool about it."

"Aha! So you do think I'm fat?" Law asked, looking mildly upset.

"Wha—?" I said, taken aback. "No! No. It's just you… I—"

Law burst out laughing. When I realized he was only teasing, I couldn't help but join in.

"You're annoying," I said, but I grinned as I did.

"Don't forget fat."

"Seriously though," I started to say. "I don't think I know anyone—our age or older—who's as cool with their body as you. How do you do it?"

"Hmm," Law mumbled as he swallowed the spoonful of rice he had just shoveled into his mouth. "I guess it helps that a lot of us in the family are the same build. My relatives talk about their health issues and my sisters laugh about outgrowing their clothes all the time. So I don't feel like I'm alone or abnormal."

"But have you ever been, y'know… bullied in school?"

"Nothing major. Little digs at my size or weight here and there," Law said, pausing to take a sip from his tumbler before he took another bite. "Maybe a few pig emoji reactions during online class the last two years."

"Is that why you eat alone here?" I blurted, immediately regretting it afterwards. It might be a sensitive issue, after all.

"Maybe. I dunno. I guess it's easier being alone sometimes."

"Yeah," I said, sighing. "I know what you mean."

"At Christmas parties, for example, I can eat so much more if I don't have to talk to anyone."

I burst out in laughter.

Law and I gobbled up the remainder of his lunch as we continued discussing the pros and cons of family gatherings.

"Well, they make the reunions more interesting, at least," Law mused.

"Who makes what interesting?" a voice behind me asked.

I looked up as Jorgia seated herself in front of Law and me, resting her chin on the back of the chair as she stared at us.

"Oh. Uhm…" Law began to mumble. The change in his expression was undeniable. From laughing and almost confident one second, he couldn't even look at Jorgia in the eyes now as he packed up his empty lunchbox. It made me wonder if Jorgia had been one of those people who teased Law about his weight.

Suddenly, I felt like I couldn't string a sentence together either. "Crass… aunts. At parties. Christmas," I stammered.

"I get you, I have a ton of those," Jorgia said, nodding. "It's all 'you look like a tomboy' or 'why aren't you on the honor roll like Jacqui?'"

I shook my head. Part of me wanted to ask Jorgia if she had someone like my Aunt Meryl, who had the nasty habit of criticizing every platter our relatives brought to our Christmas potlucks. But then I remembered that I *couldn't* be friends with her so I pursed my lips tightly instead.

There was dead air between the three of us, something that I usually hated and tried to shoo away by asking a question. But this time, I let it stay. It eventually got so awkward that Law muttered something about going to the bathroom and scuttled away.

"So, hey. I thought you were gonna go catch up with us at the caf," Jorgia said after Law had left, breaking the ice.

She sure wasn't one to shy away from difficult conversations. I felt a twinge of sadness. It would've been nice to spend more time with Jorgia and have that side of her rub off on me. She seemed a lot like how Mom might've been when she was our age.

"Anyway," Jorgia continued, not waiting for an answer, "I brought my mic. We're still recording a moody piano track for the film after school, right?"

"Oh! I totally forgot about our plans," I gasped. How could I refuse Jorgia's help now without being a total jerk?

"That's okay," Jorgia said, shrugging. "I have all the stuff we need and the music room has been reserved so we're all clear."

"Yeah except," I started, desperately wracking my brain for a decent excuse. "I have to tutor Sam after school today."

"Class has just started. What could she possibly need help with this early in the year?"

"She's… really stupid," I said weakly.

"I wouldn't have guessed it the way you talked about her wrapping your parents around her little finger," Jorgia prodded.

"Yeah well…" I began to say, inwardly hating myself for telling Jorgia so much about myself that I couldn't even lie to her. Then I had an idea, a more permanent solution to my problem: the parent card.

"Actually, Dad put me up to it." I sighed, pretending to be bummed out. "He said I needed to watch Sam everyday 'coz he'll be hella busy with work. Can you believe that?!"

"That sucks!" Jorgia looked incredulous as she hoisted herself up on the seat. But then she calmed herself down and leaned towards me, whispering in a low voice. "Okay, I'm only telling you this 'coz we're friends but, contrary to popular belief and my report card, I'm actually pretty smart. Ish. So fine, I'll help you tutor your sister if that means you can have extra time for the film. I mean, are we gonna let the man keep us from our dreams??"

As she said that last bit, Jorgia dramatically held her arms wide open. She was obviously trying to convince me but it had the opposite effect. Jorgia standing in front of me now, arms outstretched, brought back painful memories of that day when Mom had me do the same thing in front of Mai.

I stared at Jorgia, dumbstruck. She probably took it as a sign that I had agreed to her plan because she went on to show me funny videos on her phone, which she had just snuck out from underneath her blouse. She was laughing so hard that she teared up and had to wipe her eyes with her blouse collar. But I couldn't bring myself to laugh with her. I tried to focus on the screen but all I could see was Mom, pulling me by the neck my shirt and forcing me to stand in front of our house with my arms outstretched while Mai watched.

Mai, who was supposed to be my friend.

Mai, who just sat there as people called my Mom _ _ _ _ _.

If I didn't want that happening again, I had to keep to myself. If I didn't make friends and didn't let anyone get to know me, then they couldn't reject me for whose daughter I was either. Or at least, if that happened again, it wouldn't hurt as much.

"Jorgia, I'm sorry," I said over the video.

Jorgia stared at me, looking confused.

"Sorry," I repeated as I begged myself not to chicken out of saying what I was about to say next. I took a deep breath. "I know you went to all that trouble with the music room and all. But… I don't think we should work on this film together anymore."

Silence. I couldn't even look at Jorgia after I had said it. I trained my eyes on the tiled floor and just waited for her to react. It seemed like we were sitting there for ages.

"I don't get it," Jorgia finally said.

"I just… work better on my own."

There was another long pause before she spoke.

"Fine," came Jorgia's voice, the first time I've ever heard it so solemn.

Jorgia's skirt rustled against the chair as she left.

I didn't hear a single word of my teachers' lectures all afternoon. They were drowned out by the disappointment and hurt in Jorgia's voice that still rang in my ears. She would get over it faster than I would, popular as she was, I thought bitterly. I kept telling myself that it was for the best. But the sinking feeling in the pit of my stomach seemed to be telling me otherwise.

At dismissal, I packed my things up quick as lightning so I wouldn't run into Jorgia. Then I stationed myself at a discreet nook by the parking lot and decided to start on my Math homework while waiting for Dad. But after ten minutes and no progress whatsoever with my equations, I started wondering when Dad would finally arrive.

I trudged to the front gate where I knew there would be pay phones for those of us who actually bothered with the no-phone school rule. But the lone pay phone wasn't even working. Bummer, I thought as I slumped down on a bench.

Where was Dad? Had he picked Sam up yet? And if so, should I go on home or stay put? As I tried to figure out the best course of action, Mrs. Aguirre arrived at the waiting area and seated herself on the bench beside me.

"Hello, Cayt. How are you doing?" Mrs. Aguirre asked me casually as she sifted through her bulging handbag.

"I'm alright, Ma'am," was my automatic response. I watched as Mrs. Aguirre proceeded to empty the contents of her bag onto her lap and the seat between us. Was she a pack rat, I thought to myself as she pulled out receipts and folded bus tickets, candy wrappers, and wads of tissue along with two phones, an alcohol dispenser, a charger, a hairbrush, a wallet, and a bunch of pens. I edged away from her so she could have more space for her stuff. When Mrs. Aguirre started putting things back inside her bag, I suddenly remembered my situation.

"Ma'am, could I borrow your phone to call my Dad? He's supposed to pick me up."

"Of course, Cayt. Here," she said, handing me a phone with a cracked screen. "I'm really clumsy with things," she added sheepishly.

I smiled as I took her phone and dialed Dad's number. It kept ringing for a bit.

"Hello?" finally came Dad's voice.

"Dad! It's me!"

"Cayt? Oh, Cayt! Shoo—"

I heard my Dad draw a breath. "I'm so sorry, hun! I forgot all about you. I've just been swamped and… It's no excuse. I know you have a different dismissal time from Sam's—"

"So you got Sam already?"

"Yes, I meant to come back for you. Wait let me just turn off… I'll come get you now—"

"No, it's okay. I can just walk home," I said, trying not to sound disappointed.

"No, Cayt. I'll be there in a jiff," Dad insisted.

"No, it's really okay. I'll walk. You're busy there," I said.

I half expected Dad to put up a fight again, but he didn't.

"Really? Thanks, hun. You're a good girl," Dad said. "Come straight home and don't talk to strangers. Look before you cross the street—"

"I know, I know!" I said, feeling a teensy smile crawl back to my lips. "Bye, Dad."

I sighed involuntarily as I gave the phone back to Mrs. Aguirre.

"That was quite a heavy sigh, Cayt," Mrs. Aguirre said as she took her phone back.

Was it? I hadn't noticed.

"Oh, it's… nothing," I said, trying to reassure both Mrs. Aguirre and myself.

"I see. Well, I'm just here if you need anything… or nothing," Mrs. Aguirre said softly, her eyes smiling.

"I'll remember that," I said, feeling a bit nervous. I hope Mrs. Aguirre didn't see through me. "Thanks for letting me use your phone, Ma'am."

"My pleasure, Cayt. Would you like me to keep you company here?" she asked.

"Oh, no, I actually have to leave," I said, rising from my seat. With a final wave, I left Mrs. Aguirre and started walking in the direction of Elvira.

I went everywhere on my own all the time back when we were in Cauayan. And I was totally capable of going back to Elvira on my own from Lorenzo too. I even told Dad last week that he didn't need to pick me up, once I saw how close our apartment was to Lorenzo. That way, I could drop by the milk tea place or the nearby fast food chain with my classmates every once in a while. But that was when there was still a prospect of going out with classmates. Now there was none. And it sucked to be forgotten.

Stop moping, Cayt. You heard how frazzled Dad seemed. Give him a break.

Alright, alright, I sighed again.

As I kept walking, my eyes eventually landed on a bunch of kids in Lorenzo High uniforms a short distance ahead. They were clustered together and some of them were shrieking and crossing to the other side of the street or sprinting back in my direction. Probably because I was too curious for my own good, I hurried to find out what was going on.

After gaining a couple of yards, I managed to catch a glimpse of it—but immediately wished I hadn't. There, on the sidewalk, stood a man covered in a layer of dirt so thick it had become his second skin, his matted black hair grazing stiffly against his bare shoulders. It wasn't obvious at first because of the grime but, when I looked down at his pants, I realized he had none at all! The man was completely naked. And he was inching towards the Lorenzo students in front of me, his palms faced up, as if begging for alms.

I was shoved back by the small cluster of students retreating from the homeless man. Alex was one of them. She skidded past me in the direction of the school, muttering words that had been used too often to describe my mother.

_ _ _ _ _. That man.

Bagtit. My mom.

Were they one and the same?

Was my mother bound to become like this man, who couldn't even remember to put on clothes or wash his body? Was she slowly morphing into her own kind of zombie, one that didn't even have a mind of its own and had no control over its actions?

From where I stood, I took another peek at the man, careful not to look below his torso. And that was when I noticed the familiar head of black, pixie-cut hair.

Jorgia was the only student near the dirty man now, isolated as she had been by the rest of our schoolmates. I felt a panic rising inside of me, fearing that he'd hurt her or that he was sick and, since he didn't have a mask, pass the virus on to her. I waited for Jorgia to make a run for it.

But she didn't. Instead, I watched from a distance as Jorgia placed something in the man's hands. Then slowly and without much fanfare, she walked past him. As if nothing extraordinary had happened.

I shifted my eyes back to the man. He clasped both hands over whatever Jorgia had given him and stalked off calmly to the side, where he sat on a piece of cardboard. And just like that, the Lorenzo students dispersed like bubbles in the air.

Maybe I was being silly but, after seeing what I saw, I felt light as a feather. Everybody else had recoiled in fear when they saw the dirty man—everybody including me. But Jorgia was different. She was kind to him.

Maybe she would be kind to me too. And maybe she would understand and be okay with people who acted weirdly, like Mom.

I ran after Jorgia and caught up with her just as she was about to enter a coffee shop.

"Hey," I began, panting. "I'm sorry I… flaked out on you… earlier. It was really… uncool."

"No kidding," Jorgia said, her arms folded in front of her. But I thought I may have heard a chuckle when she said it, which gave me just a bit of hope.

"You probably wouldn't want to," I continued nervously, twisting the bow on the front of my school blouse between my fingers, "but I was hoping… and it's totally okay if you don't, but uhm… Can we still do the film together?"

After a few seconds, Jorgia nodded. "Okay."

My heart leaped as Jorgia's eyes curved downwards and her mask stretched over her mouth, which I knew had widened into a huge grin.

SISTERS X SECRETS

Jorgia was literally my sister from another mother.

"No, Jorg. You gotta start walking, like, right away."

We were learning *tiyakad* during third period PE and, to my surprise, I was a natural boss at walking on wooden stilts. Who would've thought? Another interesting but useless skill to add to my repertoire (aside from balancing coins on my bony fingers and getting my elbows to meet behind my back).

"Crud!" Jorg cursed as she fell off her stilt and landed on the soft grass.

"Shhh!"

I looked around to check if our PE instructor had heard but she was too busy reprimanding one of our classmates over his non-school-approved white sneakers.

"It's really simple, look," I said as I held out my stilts and wedged my right foot onto the step of the right one. After a deep breath, I quickly lifted my left leg and positioned my foot on the other stilt before walking around Jorgia in a circle, a whole foot taller than her.

"The trick is to keep moving so get off your ass," I added, laughing.

"Oh yeah?" Jorgia asked, a gleam in her eyes. She swung one of her stilts at mine. I managed to jump off just before our stilts knocked onto each other and toppled on the grass with a soft thump.

"You're such a sore loser," I teased as I bent down to pick up my stilts.

"Yeah, well you're a show-off," she answered back.

"Hey! I was just trying to help," I said. I really did want to help. It felt satisfying to actually be good at something, even though it was as impractical as walking on stilts. Also, I think my body was making up for two years without physical exercise. But did I really come across as a show-off to Jorgia? I hope not. That would be a sure AF way to become an outcast in high school.

To make absolutely certain no one, least of all Jorgia, thought I was a show-off, I stopped climbing onto the stilts and resorted to just supporting her as she teetered across the lawn on hers. But once she could walk more than five steps on her own, I figured it was safe for me to join her.

"Hey," I started to say as we wobbled towards the direction of the cafeteria. "We're still editing after school, right?"

"Yup," Jorgia said. She cursed again when she lost her footing but continued talking after I had helped her get back up on her stilts. "It's probz gonna take a while again though 'coz your audio is so dirty. I really think I should be there when you shoot next time. One crew member is better than none!"

This wasn't the first time Jorgia had offered to come over and help me with the film.

Whenever they would let me bother them, I had been shooting Dad and Sam for my zombie movie. And I really could have used Jorgia's help with lighting and, yes, sound. But just the thought of her coming over conjured in my mind one disastrous scenario after another. Dad force-feeding Jorgia animal bile in the form of *papaitan.* Sam picking her nose and licking her boogers in plain view. Mom throwing a fit and punishing me in front of Jorgia. Or worse, Mom spanking Jorgia and making *her* cry the way she did Sam before. And Jorgia's sister picking her up from our house, her short blue hair standing on end at the sight of it all.

"I know, I know," I said, keeping my eyes trained on the ground for any rocks. "My Mom just isn't… big on guests right now. Sorry."

"Menopausal?" Jorgia pried.

"No," I laughed. "But maybe something *like* that?"

"I get it. Ish. Parents—they're all weird."

"Anyway," I said, changing the subject as the bell rang for recess. "What I really need your help with is the ending."

We got off our stilts and hurried to dump them in a pile at the lawn before we headed back to our classroom to get our clothes.

"Do you think Dad and Sam should turn into zombies too? Or maybe they can escape and leave the zombie behind for another family to deal with—?"

"Or," Jorgia said, pausing for dramatic effect as we climbed the three steps from the lawn to the corridor of our building. "Maybe there's a way for them to cure the zombie! Duh!"

"A happy ending?" I asked, unconvinced. "Isn't that a bit cliché?"

"Well, you don't want to avoid a happy ending just for the sake of."

Jorgia and I turned around to see who had spoken. Our film club president, Noel, was standing with one foot propped up against the wall as he casually played with his left earlobe. He had a tiny silver stud earring in it.

"The ending has to be earned. It has to make a statement, wrap up your story," Noel continued with earnest as Jorgia and I listened on. "Not just be cool. Well, that's what I think."

"Not that we asked you to mansplain to us," Jorgia said cheekily.

"Sorry, bad habit," Noel said, grinning.

A group of seniors passed by in front of us and Noel bumped fists and exchanged complicated handshakes with a couple of boys among them, his thick mop of wavy black hair getting ruffled in the process. Once the group had left, he turned around to face us.

"Zombie film, right?" Noel asked. His nose wrinkled as he recalled this bit of information.

"Yup," Jorgia said as she squeezed my shoulder. "All those other films better watch their backs."

"Pressure much!" I hissed at her, feeling a flush rise up my cheeks. I tore my eyes away from Noel and looked down at my shoes.

"Yeah… about the booth," Noel began to say, "The good news is, if we raise enough money at the school fair, the entire film club is going to CineFiles right—?"

"This isn't news," Jorgia interrupted. She was right though, they already told us this during orientation. I looked up at Noel.

"The news is that they've added more filmmakers to the panels. Lots of women too. Jadaone, Villamor, Carolino, Swarog—"

"NO WAY. GAAAAAAH!" Jorgia and I screamed and jumped and held hands and screamed some more. We were going to meet Harriette!

Sir Li, who was on his way out of the cafeteria, gave us a funny look as he passed by. We calmed ourselves down but were still shaking with excitement when Noel spoke again.

"Right. So that's the good news," he said, hesitating.

"Wait… so there's bad news?" I asked. Were they holding it just online like last year? Or were freshmen not gonna be allowed to join in person? Could we only join if our parents went with us? 'Coz that would definitely be bad news for me.

"Well… not exactly—"

"Just spit it out already!" Jorgia demanded.

"Alright, alright," Noel said, laughing. Then he turned serious. "I did a poll on my IG stories. Apparently, nobody wants to pay to watch a bunch of student films! _ _ _ _, huh? They all wanna tape Mrs. Castro to the wall, that sort of thing. So. No money…"

"No Swag," I finished for him, feeling like I had just thrown away a winning lottery ticket.

Jorgia and I looked at each other in horror.

"On the bright side, though," Noel continued, clapping his hands, "more room for ideas! I'm sure you have a lot of those. So just DM me whenever."

With a casual wave, Noel sauntered off into the cafeteria. Jorgia and I went back on our way to our classroom.

"Dude, slow down," I heard Jorgia pant from behind me. "What's up with you?"

"Huh? What do you mean?"

"Why are you walking so fast?"

"Oh, was I?" I asked, coming to. We were only a few feet away from our room. I made a conscious effort to match Jorgia's pace as we went inside and grabbed our uniforms off the backs of our seats. The room was empty so we decided to get dressed right there.

"You're acting really weird," Jorgia continued as she pulled her T-shirt off and wiggled into her blouse.

"No, I'm not," I said as I did the same.

"Sure. You're *not* acting weird. Your face is just red as a tomato for no reason," she added, a glint in her eyes.

On instinct, I felt my face with my palms.

Jorgia burst out laughing. I threw my sweaty T-shirt at her but it fell a foot short, which just made her laugh even louder.

"Will you quit it!" I hissed, rolling my eyes as I picked my shirt back up and stuffed my things inside my bag. "Aren't you worried about the booth?"

"Yeah, but it's not as if we're gonna die if we don't win or we don't get to go to CineFiles," Jorgia said. "There's always next year."

Maybe I was overreacting. Or acting weird, like Jorgia said. I definitely felt weird, like my body couldn't decide what was happening inside it. Was I anxious that I had acted like a dork in front of Noel? Self-conscious that Jorgia might have noticed?

Or was I stressed out about potentially failing to meet the one person I looked up to right now?

"We need to meet Swarog!"

"Okay! Okay," Jorgia said.

"How are we gonna do it?" I wondered aloud. "Wanna search for ideas after we edit?"

"Sure. But I doubt if we can find the answer just by scrolling through YouTube while we render, you know? We need to look where nobody else is looking."

"Like the library?" I suggested, remembering how deserted it was when I hid there.

"The wha—? Oh, right. No! I dunno, the streets, maybe? My parents always told me you could find inspiration in the most ordinary places if you cared enough to look."

"Deep," I said as I ripped a pack of crackers open and offered it to Jorgia.

"Yeah they also said commercial toothpaste is bad for you. So it's fifty-fifty with those two, really," Jorgia said, chuckling as she took a cracker. "Anyway, our street is pretty busy so it'll be a good place to people-watch and figure out this booth thing. Come over later!"

"To your house?" I asked, nibbling on a cheese cracker.

"Duh. Yeah. My parents have a meeting at Paradiso though so don't expect anything but instant noodles 'coz that's all I can cook. But if my *ate*'s there, maybe we can get her to order us pizza or something."

"I dunno… I'll have to ask my Dad first."

I was pretty sure Dad couldn't care less. In fact, I'd bet my phone passcode that he'd like nothing more than to have one less kid in the house, even for just an afternoon. Even though I've been helping out at home a lot, like with dinner prep and the laundry and Sam's homework and all that, I think Dad still gets stressed whenever he sees me holding a knife the wrong way or whenever Sam complains to him that I'm a bossy tutor. But I wasn't sure I could survive another close call with Jorgia's sister without her recognizing me.

"He, uh… might not approve of having just a college student in the house with us," I continued to say. "Especially if you think she could be smoking pot or something."

"That was a joke, Cayt! And even if it weren't, the trick is to *not* tell your Dad."

"Okay, I won't. But, hey!" I said, a lightbulb suddenly switching on in my head. "Why don't we just go to Paradiso instead? Maybe that's just as good a place to get inspired. I mean, Maginhawa street is pretty busy too, right?"

Jorgia looked at me like I was a genius. And, to be honest, I felt pretty good about myself too. Crisis averted.

Jorgia and I bumped fists just as the bell for fourth period rang. In a matter of seconds, our classmates started streaming back into the room. I looked at the packet on the desk between me and Jorgia and saw that there was one last piece left. I made to reach for it but Jorgia snatched it from between my fingers.

"Hey!" I choked.

"Can I have it?" Jorgia asked, stuffing it whole into her mouth before I could answer.

"Pathetic," I said, laughing. I rolled my eyes at her one last time and, slipping my mask back on, sidled into my seat beside Law just as Mrs. Aguirre entered the room.

Almost every day, I had to come up with some fresh excuse or plan to avoid running into Jorgia's sister and keep both of them from seeing my Mom too. And every day, I grew more and more uneasy about it, like what I was doing was wrong, or that all my lies were bound to catch up with me someday.

It wasn't that I didn't trust Jorgia to be kind. That moment with the _ _ _ _ _ man on the street was proof that she wouldn't be mean or grossed out by people who were different from her or whom she didn't understand. But I liked how things were between us now. We were equals. We could be nice to each other, but we also felt comfortable enough to swing a stilt at the other person. I just wanted for us to be actual friends—and not for me to be some charity case that she'd feel sorry for or feel obliged to be nice to. So, I intended to keep Mom a secret for as long as I could manage it.

Even sisters and friends kept secrets from each other, right?

OUT OF CHARACTER

Things at school and with Jorgia were nearly perfect but, at home, nothing was as it should be.

Sure, Mom no longer stayed in bed all day. But I think I preferred that Mom over the current one who gets triggered by every little thing. Some days, Mom swept through the house like a hurricane, leaving behind a path of destruction wherever she went.

We hadn't even finished the breakfast Dad had had delivered to our doorstep early Sunday morning, but he was already buried in paperwork. He had taken on more clients in the past month to keep up with our expenses and kept stepping out of the house for calls every fifteen minutes or so (we had very bad reception inside). Meanwhile, Mom was actually helping Sam out with her schoolwork for once. Or more like Mom was doing the watercolor painting by herself after having shooed Sam away to the other end of the table so my sister wouldn't end up ruining her own project. It was all a bit chaotic, but the kind that was probably normal for families who were still getting used to not having any help.

Seeing opportunity in adversity, I decided to be the good kid Dad kept reminding Sam and me to be so Mom would stay in a happy mood. As soon as I finished my homework, I went back downstairs and volunteered to do the laundry. For free. That, in itself, should've earned me a few votes toward teen canonization.

But no. What I got instead for trying to help out were stained blouses and a verbal beating from my own mother.

"For chrissak—CAYT! You mixed the coloreds with the whites!" Mom shrieked when I crawled into the kitchen to show her the clothes I had accidentally turned blue. She got up so fast, she knocked over a cup, spilling gray liquid all over the table.

"I didn't," was all I managed to whisper as Mom swore angrily and hastily mopped up the mess. I got really tongue-tied whenever I was nervous. And angry zombie Mom made me very nervous.

I followed Mom back to the adjacent laundry room and watched as she burrowed through the washing machine, unearthing stained shirt after stained shirt. Finally, she fished out a blue tie-dyed scarf that I had never seen before.

"My project!" Sam gasped behind me.

"What project?" I asked.

"What is it doing here?" Mom asked the same time I spoke, waving the scarf violently at Sam's nose. My sister shriveled under Mom's stare.

"You said to wash it," Sam squeaked as she looked down at her feet. "So I put it in the basket 'coz *ate* was—"

"Me?!"

"Will you stop and let her finish?!" Mom shouted, grabbing me by my shirt sleeve.

"Hey! HEY!"

I turned around to see Dad staring at us.

"Everything alright in here?" Dad asked, a note of caution in his voice.

Sam and I immediately came to our senses, but not Mom.

"Oh grrrreat! Everything's just great, Eric. As you can see, the kitchen's a mess, our clothes are ruined. Oh, and our daughters don't know how to use their brains, apparently," Mom spat, her words slicing through me like knives. She shoved the tie-dyed scarf against my chest and stormed out of the room.

The sound of a door slamming just seconds later told me that she had locked herself up in their room again. Sam started bawling, forcing Dad to put down his phone and wrap his arms around Sam.

"Don't listen to your Mom. She's just very emotional right now," Dad said as he rubbed Sam's back. "Mind telling me what happened here, Cayt?"

I told him all that had gone down, with emphasis on the fact that it was Sam's scarf that *she* had placed in the basket that ruined everything, and that I now had only one white blouse (my back-up) left and five days of school coming up.

"I can just run them on another cycle and add bleach, don't worry abut it."

"If it's that easy, then why was Mom so upset?" I asked.

I had been trying to bury the growing sense of dread over the past months that, just maybe, those people back in Cauayan were right. That there was something wrong with Mom, something that couldn't be cured by pretending everything was normal or trying to be impossibly perfect.

"Dad, don't you think Mom needs help? Like therapy, or medication? Something!"

Dad let out a heavy sigh and told Sam to brush her teeth, waiting until she was out of earshot before he answered me.

"Cayt, I know what you're trying to say but it's not that simple. Mom's… not ready yet."

"Well how is she gonna be ready? And what are we gonna do in the meantime?"

Like clockwork, Dad's phone started vibrating on the kitchen table. He checked who it was before ignoring the call. Then Dad turned to me again, giving my shoulder a gentle squeeze as he sat me down on a chair. He pulled up another chair and seated himself across me, our knees practically touching.

"Cayt, we can't force Mom to do something she doesn't want to do," Dad said, leaning forward as he spoke. "So we're gonna have to try to be more patient, okay?"

Dad gave me a smile that seemed to say, "Sorry, I know it's hard but this is the only way."

I couldn't summon a smile back.

"Hey, I know what else we can do to help," Dad said, grinning.

"What?" I asked, curious.

"Not mix the coloreds with the whites," he chuckled. "Ha! Get it?"

I don't know what it was just then. My rational side was fully aware that Dad was teasing. This was how we were, him and I. I've always liked that we could just poke fun at each other. But at that moment, I just lost it.

"I didn't do it!" I growled, knocking down my chair as I stood. "It was totally Sam's fault."

"Whoa. Calm down, Cayt. I was just joking," Dad said, looking straight at me with his hands up in the air, as if in surrender.

"I know it's not your fault. But there's no need to point fingers. Sam's just a kid, after all."

I searched Dad's eyes. There was no anger in them, not like Mom's. But I couldn't understand why he didn't seem to feel sorry for me or why he couldn't get why I was upset. Where was my pity hug? Where was my free pass for making a mistake?

"Well so am I!" I shouted.

Without even realizing that I was doing it, I did a Mom and stormed out of the room, making as loud a din as I could as I climbed up the spiral staircase and shut myself inside Sam's and my room.

On most days, I couldn't wait to grow up so I could start working in film, make my own money, even drive and drink (though not at the same time), or just go out without having to ask for permission. But the way Dad talked to me, it was like I couldn't afford to mess up even the little things anymore. I wasn't sure if I was ready for that kind of growing up just yet.

I stayed in bed past noon, ignoring Dad's messages that it was time to eat. I waited for him to come up to our room, undecided what I would do or how I'd respond when he did—but he didn't. And neither did Sam. Good. Woe was her if she had.

A quarter to three o'clock in the afternoon, Dad texted to ask me if I was going to mass with them. I paused long and hard before typing back.

No.

Three wiggling dots appeared. I waited anxiously for the dots to morph into letters. Was he going to reprimand me for not going to church? Or maybe apologize for his behavior?

Finally, a swoosh told me he had sent the message. It was a long and detailed instruction for reheating the *arroz caldo* they had for lunch, with options for doing it in the microwave or on stovetop.

I pressed my face down on my pillow and let it muffle my scream.

It was a good thing I had school the very next day because I was getting claustrophobic, restricted as I was to my and Sam's room. I hated sneaking off to the kitchen and being caught by Dad stealing snacks from the pantry or the fridge to make up for the meals I didn't eat with them.

Dad dropped me off in front of school in the morning before he did Sam.

"Don't pick me up," I said bluntly as I made to get my allowance from Dad's hands. He snatched it back just in time.

"Why not?" he asked. It was the first time we had said anything to each other in person.

I pried the bills from Dad's hand and mumbled "school project" so he couldn't object. Without another word, I climbed out of our car, slamming the door behind me.

My zombie movie was technically a school project now since we were submitting it to film club. I was supposed to shoot the last scenes over the weekend but really couldn't bring myself to ask Dad for help. So I had to improvise. No biggie. I bet Swarog had to deal with stuff like this all the time.

"You can't recast your main characters when you're about to get to the ending!"

Jorgia and I were standing in line for pizza during lunch and I had just finished telling her the plan. She shook her head so hard, her bangs got all messed up.

"Just kiss and make up with him already."

One of the lunch ladies clucked at us as she handed Jorgia her order. I ignored her.

"I am *not* apologizing."

"Why are you so angry with him anyway?"

I had been asking myself that question too. I mean, it was Mom who had called me stupid. And it was Sam who got me in trouble. But all of that, I was used to. With Dad, though, I was expecting more. He was supposed to understand. He was supposed to be on my side too. It hurt that he wasn't.

"Dad told me off for something that was Sam's fault," I said, not wanting to elaborate.

"Ugh. Parents," Jorgia chimed in. "Mine play faves too. Ish. Though I'd be less annoyed about it if I were the favorite."

I chuckled. Then we sat in silence for a few seconds as we gobbled up our pizzas.

"You can't play his part though," I said, casually scanning the room. My eyes fell on Law.

"Yeah, well, nobody said I was perfect." Jorgia said, sticking her tongue out at me.

"Maybe we can ask Law," I said. It was just a wacky idea but literally two seconds later—

"HEY LAW! COME OVER HERE!" Jorgia shouted at him from across the room. Several students sitting nearby looked disapprovingly at us and a handful quickly slipped their masks on.

"What the heck? You can't just make him come over like that," I hissed at Jorgia under my breath.

"Yeah?" Law asked as he ambled over, looking confused.

"Can you star in our student film?" Jorgia asked.

Law looked curiously at us. "I thought you guys were nearly done with that," he said.

Before I could answer, Jorgia blurted out, "Yeah but we can't finish shooting with Cayt's Dad because they're on cold war right now—"

"You don't need to announce it to everybody," I said, fuming.

"Sor-ry. Sheesh," Jorgia said, not sounding the least bit apologetic. She turned back to Law. "So, will you?"

"Okay," he said, simple as that.

And that was how Jorg, Law, and I spent the next few days after school—shooting the ending to our movie.

Our film club president had said that the ending should make a statement. And this was mine: if you let a zombie roam around your house unchecked for too long, the odds are that it'll get to you and turn you into a zombie too. This family didn't do enough when they still had the chance—and now they were paying the price. But it wasn't a super sad ending; the Dad still manages to save his kid before he meets his end.

We were about to film the part where Dad's character was slowly transforming into a monster. Law, his face and hands completely zombified, emerged from the boys' restrooms wearing the clothes Jorgia had artfully shredded. He crept towards us slowly, twisting the joints of his body as he did so that it looked like they were broken in places.

"Aaack!" Jorgia squealed, laughing as she ran away.

I couldn't help but clap. "You're a natural, Law!"

Law broke out of character and, grinning, bowed and said, "Thanks."

"How did you get so good at this?" I asked him as we walked to the storage room, where we would be shooting the last scene.

"I dunno. I like copying moves, I guess," Law said, shrugging. Then he added, "I dance sometimes, when I'm alone."

"Really?!" I asked, taken aback. I wouldn't have guessed that about Law. People can be surprising.

For the second time that afternoon, we filmed Law writhing and growling in pain, his hands tied to an exposed pipe from which he was struggling to break free. I got goosebumps when we played back our footage. Because Jorgia and I had used very minimal lighting and shot either silhouettes or extreme close-ups of Law's hands, mouth, and eyes, I think there was a real chance of pulling off the casting change!

After we got a random third grader with curly hair like Sam's to run away from us as we filmed her, we finally called it a wrap. To celebrate, the three of us laid on the grass, munching on cheese fries from the canteen.

"These things taste like cardboard," I complained.

"Don't stuff them into your mouth then," Jorgia said, sticking her orange tongue out at me.

"You know the old nuns' home by the ballet rooms?" Law asked. "You can buy potato wedges there. They're really good. Made with love."

"Hey!" I said, propping myself up on one elbow. "I've heard about those mystery fries! How come we've never tried them?"

"'Coz the grade schoolers clean them out before we make it to last period," Jorgia said.

"I miss grade school," Law sighed. "The subjects were easier then."

"I just miss those fries," Jorgia said. "And school ending at three. Those were the good ol' days!" Jorgia said the last line with relish, brandishing a french fry between her fingers like a cigarette.

We laughed at her and continued to eat our subpar fries until it was time for us to pack up and go home for the weekend.

I was dreading being stuck with only my family for two whole days but my group chats with Jorgia and Law kept me afloat. They especially came in handy when, after receiving the good news from Noel, I felt so happy that I even decided to call a truce with Dad.

"Dad! DAD!" I shouted as I burst into the kitchen, where I knew he'd be. "They're gonna show our film at school!"

Dad didn't even look up from the ledgers spread across the table.

"Hellooo! Did you hear me?" I asked, waving my hands in front of Dad's face as I sat on one of the dining chairs, excited to talk to him.

"Not now, Cayt," was all he said as he sifted through the books.

Feeling dejected, I got back on my feet and made my way out of the kitchen. As I closed the door behind me, I said, "I thought you should know… they really liked your performance."

Then I ran up to my room, ready to cry into or punch my pillow or both. But my phone was buzzing with a million messages.

Jorgia: AMFSJHDGS!!! I TOLDJUUU <3 <3 <3

Law: Congrats, Cayt and Jorg! *clap*

Jorgia: slaaaay

At least some things were as they should be.

TALKIE

I could really use someone to talk to.

Every now and then, I'd feel something from within my chest vaguely telling me to just 'fess up to Jorg or even Law already. Sometimes, it was a warmth that spread from my neck up to my face and down to my toes, reassuring me that the gravitational pull that held us together would stay intact—even with a Mom or other issues like mine. That they were people around whom I could be myself completely.

Other times, it would feel as if two invisible, freakishly big hands had wrapped themselves around my ribs, squeezing me tight—and the only way I could breathe again was if I spilled all my secrets.

And once or twice, I almost did. Luckily, I was pretty good at holding my breath. Otherwise, I might've cracked when, on the very morning that I was supposed to leave early for the class trip, Mom misplaced my permission slip.

"I thought I had filed it with the mail. Ooh! Maybe it's in Dad's work folders?" Mom chirped as she darted from one end of the living room to the other, tearing the place apart.

"Why is this happening to me?!" I cried. The time on my phone leapt forward by a minute.

"Calm down, Cayt," Dad said. He started scribbling haphazardly on a paper towel. "I'm writing you a waiver now, see?"

"Wait! Maybe it's in the kitchen," Mom said as she disappeared into the other room.

"Don't bother, hon!" Dad shouted after her, folding up the makeshift permission slip and grabbing the car keys from the table. "We're leaving!"

Without waiting for Mom to acknowledge, Dad and I sprinted out of the house.

"Why can't she let me be happy for once?" I blurted out.

"Cayt! Don't let your Mom hear you talking about her like that," Dad said, dead serious. "She'll get upset."

"I don't give a sh—" I had started to say but stopped mid-curse when I saw the look on my Dad's face.

Even though I had warped into a great big ball of fury and nerves by that moment, I still had the tiniest sense to know that Dad should never be crossed when his eyes were bloodshot and his forehead, a weave of wrinkles. I clamped my mouth shut and parked my ass in the car, praying to God almighty during the drive to Lorenzo that I would still make it.

We got there just before the chartered bus could make it out past the school gates. Good thing too 'coz I don't know what I would've done otherwise. I boarded the bus in a hurry, holding back my tears as I looked for where Jorgia and Law were seated, waiting for me.

"Don't you wish we were here to watch a musical instead?" Jorgia asked as we alighted the bus in front of the cultural center. "It would be so cool if they played Hamilton!"

I didn't answer. I was too busy taking in the sight of the giant, floating, square-shaped structure up close for the first time. It looked like a U.F.O. with sharp corners. Our class filed in line, flashing our vaccination cards before we could pass through security. We climbed up a short set of stairs and spilled into a high-ceilinged lobby with plush red carpeting and a grand staircase that spiraled onto an upper level.

Mrs. Aguirre gave a short spiel about Mental Health Awareness Day then instructed us to view and reflect on the exhibits at our own pace while observing proper museum etiquette. After the class dispersed, Jorgia and I wandered off to a dimly-lit corner where a bunch of benches surrounded a bamboo tree with paper cranes for leaves.

Along a nearby wall were a couple of shelves that held glass bottles of different shapes and sizes, strips of paper nestled within each of them. Jorgia and I held our noses close to the bottles, taking turns reading the poems inside out loud.

"'When my mask shatters and you see how… *grower? Grocer??* I really am…' That doesn't sound right," I said, squinting.

Jorgia nudged me to the side and recited the rest of it as if she were at a poetry slam.

"'When my mask

shatters

and you see

how broken

I really am

will you

S-T-I-L-L

love me?'"

Jorgia fake bowed and waved off imaginary compliments in the air as I re-read the poem to myself.

I wasn't sure if a sentence arranged like a poem could actually be considered a poem in English class. But I was pretty sure that whoever wrote this poem was neither the first nor the last person to ask this question. I asked myself the same thing almost every day. But just in a less fancy way.

"Sheesh. Why are these poems so dark?" Jorgia asked from behind me.

I noticed a table beside the shelves of bottles and saw that there was more information there about *Julia's Bench*. I skimmed the text until—

"'…the things she left behind.' I think she killed herself," I said, but more to myself than to Jorgia.

"What?" Jorgia asked, distracted. She had been struggling to fold a paper crane following a set of instructions on the wall. She cast what looked more like a paper boat aside and started reading the poster too.

"Ohh. That's sad."

I nodded as I moved away from the table and wandered towards the benches, counting if there were eighteen like the poster said. Eighteen benches for eighteen years of life.

I examined the ones surrounding the paper crane tree, some of which had poems etched in hidden corners, echoing the voice of the girl trapped inside the glass bottles. One was bright red and didn't look sad at all. Another had large round beads glued all over it in a polka dot pattern, which must make it a very prickly and uncomfortable bench to sit on. A bit ironic, considering that these benches, in particular, were made for sitting on by people who needed someone to talk to.

Would it work? I wondered.

I scanned the room for the best bench to sit on but they had all been occupied by rowdy schoolmates or a few grown-ups who looked at the paper-crane tree with such laser focus, you'd think they were meditating for finals.

Determined, I sat on the prickly bench, waiting.

The surface really was uncomfortable. Like when you get pebbles in your shoe—only this time, it was beads in the seat of your pants.

I jumped as I felt the weight of a hand on my shoulder.

"We are not leaving until I make at least one," Jorgia said, tossing a stack of origami paper at me. She sat on the floor and started folding. I took a sheet and did the same. In no time at all, I had one, then another. When I noticed that Jorgia was still struggling with her first, I moved from the bench to the floor and helped her out with her origami.

"Hey! You never told me you had a knack for this sort of stuff," Jorgia said.

"Thanks," I said, my voice cracking.

Then *it* started again. There was a loud ringing between my ears. My ribs were contracting, squeezing my lungs so they would press into my heart and force me to squeal. I balled my hands into fists and pounded my chest as I coughed, willing for *it* to go away.

"Are you okay?" Jorgia asked, looking alarmed.

I gasped for air and tried to croak "yeah" but no sound came out from between my lips. Alright, alright! I'm gonna do it! The moment I said it to myself, my lungs cleared up and I could breathe and see clearly again. I think it meant my body thought this was the right thing.

Jorgia was looking at me funny.

I didn't say anything. Instead, I got up and placed our paper cranes next to each other at the base of the tree. Then I sat back down next to Jorgia and took a deep breath.

"Have I ever told you about my Mom?"

So I did. Not all of it. Not about the pills, because I still remember how Dad said nobody else should know about it. But I told Jorg about the last few days and how Mom's been weird and unpredictable and infuriating like that ever since Miggy died. How she was usually either sad zombie Mom or angry zombie Mom, and only normal happy Mom on rare occasions. I even shared my theory about her having bipolar disorder.

"Whoa," Jorgia said, letting out a low whistle.

"Isn't this the kind of talk people have over beers?" I asked to lighten the mood.

Jorgia chuckled before going silent. When she spoke again, it was more serious.

"I'm so sorry, Cayt. That's… that must be tough shiz."

"What's tough shiz?" Law's voice came from behind us.

I panicked, wondering if Law had heard. I caught Jorgia's eyes and could've sworn she was thinking the same thing. Good thing she was much more quick-witted than me.

"Dysmenorrhea," she said to Law, rolling her eyes at him as she got up from the floor.

"Forget I asked," Law said, suddenly looking very uncomfortable.

"Do you have it too? Is that why you took so long in there?" Jorgia prodded him. "Or were you dancing in front of the bathroom mirror again?"

Law's ears turned pink and gave him away.

"Your secret's safe with us," I said affectionately to Law as we laughed and followed the rest of our schoolmates back to the bus.

Once we had parked ourselves into a row near the back of the vehicle, Jorgia wiggled her eyebrows at me and Law, and whispered so nobody else could hear.

"So, remember what we were talking about earlier?"

"No—" I said quickly, my eyes boring into Jorgia's.

"What?" Law asked at the same time.

"Cayt was thinking about having a beer," Jorgia whispered, a mischievous gleam in her eyes.

"No I wasn't!" I said, both relieved and taken aback by what Jorgia was suggesting.

"Will you be quiet?" Jorgia hissed, craning her neck to check if the students in the seats nearby were paying us any attention. They were mostly on their phones. We put our heads together again.

"I know a store a few blocks off Lorenzo. My sister used to drag me along when she bought drinks for her parties."

Without a moment's hesitation, Law said, "I'm in."

"Alright, Law! Cayt? G?"

I looked up to make sure that Mrs. Aguirre was far away, still talking with our other classmates who were unlucky enough to get stuck in the front rows. I was pretty sure there was something in the student handbook about drinking at our age. If not in there, then the Philippine Constitution or something. But I wasn't gonna chicken out—not when it seemed like Jorgia was actually doing this for me, to help me. And who knows? Maybe it would.

"Just make sure we don't get caught," I said.

As an extra precaution, we waited fifteen minutes after most of our teachers and classmates had left school before we headed off to the Korean grocery store nearby. Jorgia made Law and me stand outside while she procured our drinks because "you guys actually look like you're fourteen," she had said. After a moment, she emerged from the store with three fruit ice pops and a bottle of soju.

Law and I gave her a funny look.

"That's it?" I asked.

"You'll take what I give and thank me for it," Jorgia said as we strolled down the street.

"I thought you and your sister bought drinks here all the time?" Law accused Jorgia.

"New cashier," Jorgia groaned, twisting the bottle open and handing it to me.

Aware that Law and Jorg were watching me, I slipped off my mask and took a sip of the clear liquid, careful not to touch the bottle with my mouth. The soju wasn't strong but still had an aftertaste that I didn't like. "*Bleaaaagh.*"

"Pathetic," Jorgia teased, grabbing the green bottle from my hand and taking a swig. "You know this is actually sweet compared to a lot of drinks, right?"

Law took a huge gulp, to my and Jorgia's amazement. He shrugged. "My papa's a drunk."

Jorgia and I stared at each other and shuffled our feet as we turned the corner, looking for something to say. Then Law burst out laughing, nearly spraying us with drool.

"Gotcha!"

We laughed and punched and fake-choked Law for a few seconds. Then we ate our ice pops and, after finishing the soju, rid ourselves of the evidence in the nearest trash can. I had to admit that, although it was pretty exciting to do something kinda forbidden like that, I wasn't in a hurry to drink again no matter what Jorgia said.

We stopped by a Jollibee 'coz Law had to use the bathroom (twice!), then grabbed a taxi to drop us all off. On the way to Law's house, Jorgia kept teasing Law about his bladder issue. "You barely had two sips, you baby!" Jorgia roared between her and my guffaws.

"S'not true! I'm bigger than you two so the volume of my sips is naturally larger too. I probably had, hmm, how much was in that bottle again, oh yeah, one, two hundred milliliters?" Law said, barely stopping for a breath. "So I had at least a hundred of that stuff. Oh, man. I think I'm getting tipsy too."

This made Jorgia and me giggle even more. Who knew Law could be so talkie?

We arrived at Law's and waited for him to get inside before making our way to mine. Then it began to dawn on me what we did.

It was one thing to have a sip of alcohol at family gatherings and under the supervision of older relatives. It was another thing entirely to have done it with friends after a school trip. I breathed heavily into the inside of my mask several times, sniffing the air for the tiniest whiff of alcohol. I shook Jorgia's arm.

"Jorg, smell your breath! I feel like mine smells like soju."

"Stop shaking me!"

Jorg was squirming and looked very uncomfortable, her muscles all tensed up.

"I need to pee," she said, sucking in a deep breath.

"Okay," I said. "Let's ask the driver… Kuya, can we go to—"

"No! Your house is two minutes away. I needed to go two seconds ago."

"But Jorg—" I blubbered, remembering who was waiting for me at home. I had literally just told her about Mom—that didn't mean she had to experience her firsthand.

"Shhh. I need peace. Shh," Jorgia said, closing her eyes tight as if to meditate.

The facade of Elvira came into view and, begrudgingly, I asked our driver to slow down. As soon as the car stopped, Jorgia shot out of the door and onto the sidewalk, her legs quivering while she stood outside our apartment. As she whispered, "come on, come on, come on," between sharp breaths, I finally got a grasp of the urgency of the situation.

Okay, fine! Let her see Mom. I scrambled for my keys inside my school bag.

"Cayt! Hurry!" Jorgia shrieked, a note of terror in her voice.

"Wait a sec!" I said, getting on my knees and emptying the contents of my bag onto the pavement. I kept my eyes peeled for the familiar glint of brass.

"Fuuudge, I gotta go!" I heard Jorgia say just as my fingers clasped over cold metal.

"Here!" I shouted as I turned around, only to see Jorgia hop onto the tiny patch of greenery in front of our unit and squat there, half-hidden by my Dad's *calamansi* shrubs.

There was total silence between us, punctuated only by a long tinkling sound.

Then Jorgia got up, stepped out from behind the shrubs and, calm as can be, asked, "Now, can I use your bathroom?"

I lifted my jaws from where it had dropped on the floor and whispered, "Dude, you just peed on my Dad's plants."

"I'm trying not to think about it."

"I can't unsee it. It's permanently etched into my memory," I said, still in shock. "We're, like, bonded for life… Well, you, me, and our kuya driver," I added, remembering the taxi parked across the street.

"Shut up and lend me some pants," Jorgia hissed, walking past me to the front door.

I went quiet as I unlocked the door, worried that I had crossed the line.

When we were finally making our way inside, Jorgia spoke up. "I'm never teasing Law about using the bathroom again. Talk about bad karma."

I laughed so hard, my face grew hot. It was a warmth that spread from my face and neck, down to my toes.

BFFS (AGAIN)

When I was eight, Mom promised me we'd always be best friends.

Sam was just about to be born then and I can't remember much of it now, but I guess I was acting all stupid and jealous or something. I vaguely remember locking myself up in the room and refusing to let Dad and Ate Fe bring Sam's crib inside. Yeah, I had probably said that I had wanted a sibling. I mean, I must've already known then that having one would mean sharing everything and everyone with him or her. But I guess I had thought it would be even, you know? I had hated how Mom started turning me down when I wanted her and me to read books and act out the scenes in my room because she was too tired and needed to rest so Sam would be healthy. So I must've thought that if I could keep Sam's crib out, my parents couldn't possibly have her.

Like I said, I was eight.

But Mom figured it out. She still paid attention then. With my flimsy bedroom door between us, she calmed me down and told me that, even though Sam was coming and of course she and Dad would love her to pieces, they would always love me as much. Hearts weren't like houses, she had said, where you had to make room for new furniture by getting rid of old ones or else

144

they'd be really cramped and uncomfortable and look more like a bodega than a home. No, hearts were like the big old mango tree in the middle of our farm—me and all of my cousins and even our heavyset Titos could all climb it at the same time and still, it wouldn't run out of sturdy branches for us to sit on. Instead it would just grow and grow as it had for almost a hundred years, and keep bearing its sweet, golden fruit.

And that was how Mom convinced me to open up my room and my heart to Sam.

I was so attached to Mom then.

It was kinda sad, now that I thought about it. Especially since Mom probably didn't know or care a thing about me now. Whenever she looked at me, I could feel that all she saw were the mistakes I unintentionally kept making. Other times, she just looked past me like I didn't exist or, worse, didn't matter. It didn't feel like she was a mom to me at all, much less a best friend.

But after our class trip, the thought didn't make me as sad because, at least, now I had Jorgia.

I had been so worried when I let her inside our house after our class trip. And when Dad saw that I had brought a friend, he seemed a little surprised too. We hadn't opened up our home (neither here nor in Cauayan) to people outside our family in a while. But Jorgia was really nice. Mind, she was gonna borrow clean pants so she had to be. But she laughed at most of Dad's jokes and even posted a video of Sam and her on her TikTok. *And* she acted like it was totally normal when Mom tried to cook up a storm only to end up burning everything so that we had to order pizza for dinner instead.

We never brought up my Mom or Jorgia's accident when we were with Law or the others. But on occasion, and when it was just us, Jorgia would either poke fun at her incident or ask me how things were at home—and I'd know that we had become best friends.

One afternoon after class, Jorgia and I went to the basement canteen and found ourselves face to face with Noel.

"Spill. Whatcha got for me?" Noel asked.

"Uhm… hotel toothbrushes, canned sardines… and girls' clothes," I stammered as I snuck the quickest peek at our club president, who was manning the typhoon relief donations table.

"And—a place in Binondo that delivers Soup No. Five," Jorgia added, grinning.

"Sorry what's that again?" Noel asked as he tossed our donations into cardboard boxes.

"Cow genitals," Jorgia said, all business-like.

Noel's eyes lit up.

"That is OG! You guys just made my day. Our booth is going to be—" Noel trailed off, bumping fists with us instead.

Just then, a couple more students approached the table, dragging a whole sack of goods behind them. Jorgia and I rushed to help Noel segregate their donations.

Seeing as nobody wanted to pay to watch our films, we decided to play a game in between the screenings to raise money at the school fair. The film club would get faculty and popular (or infamous) students to answer potentially embarrassing questions—for a price to be paid by the student body. It would be a spin on a game called "Spill Your Guts or Fill Your Guts" on this late night comedy show that Jorgia's sister loved watching and got her hooked into as well.

For our school fair version, students needed to contribute to the total bid on the players of their choice and only if the total amount was raised would their chosen player take the spot against a film club member. The players would then take turns asking the other incriminating questions and, if they didn't want to answer, they had to eat really gross stuff like Soup No. Five. And, just like our short films, the game would be streamed live online and on a wide screen at the school lawn. It was going to be massive.

"So who've you got signed up to spill their guts yet?" Jorgia asked.

"We've got Aguirre and Li—easy enough. Though Sir Li did try to bribe me into making sure durian wasn't on the table when he takes his turn. We'll see about that," Noel winked as he arranged packs of instant noodles neatly inside one of the boxes. "There are a lot more slots to fill but, for our finale, we got Mrs. Castro."

"What?!" I squealed. "That is… insane."

"No effing way!" Jorgia said at the same time.

I bet anybody who'd ever been sent to the disciplinary office would want to see Mrs. Castro choking on cow testicles. Although, from my encounter with her, she didn't seem like half the satanic witch some people have made her out to be. Or like she could be threatened with a handful of animal organs.

"CineFiles, here we come!" Noel said, bumping fists with us again. "You guys are Swags, right?"

I nodded, surprised that he knew how Swarog's devoted fans called ourselves.

"Cool, you've got good taste… for freshmen, at least," Noel said, chuckling.

My cheeks felt warm as Jorgia and I walked away.

Literally just thirty seconds later, Jorgia, in a sickeningly syrupy sweet voice, started teasing me. "Somebody's a mess around No-el!"

"Shh!" I said, my body doing a 360-degree turn to make sure absolutely no one had heard that. My heart jumped at the sight of a group of seniors in the butterfly garden just a few meters from us. Thankfully, they seemed to be focused on their watercolors.

"I am not," I said as I kept walking.

"Is that right? Maybe we should go back and help him out then?" Jorgia asked, turning around and retracing her steps.

"No!" I said, grabbing Jorgia and pulling her in the opposite direction. She laughed like a monkey and teased me all the way to the front gate and as we were climbing into their car.

"What are you girls giggling about?" Jorgia's mom asked by way of greeting as she peered at us from the top of her round, rose-tinted sunglasses.

"Nothing *po*," Jorgia and I hurriedly answered as we piled into the backseat. I took the back of Jorg's mom's hand and pressed it briefly on my forehead.

"I get it. Boys, huh?" Jorgia's mom said, winking.

"No!" Jorgia shrieked. "Mom, mind your own biz please."

"Well you *are* my business. You girls are way too young to have boyfriends—"

"It's just a crush," I found myself defending.

"Aha! So you admit it," Jorg said, beaming.

I pretended to not have heard her and instead pursed my lips to keep me from incriminating myself any further. Meanwhile, as Jorgia's mom continued to talk a mile a minute, the front door opened and Jorgia's sister slipped into the passenger's seat holding a cup of fishballs, her blue hair styled in place with a fabric headband.

My heart missed a couple of beats. I thought Jorgia's mom was picking us up because her sister couldn't?

I was okay with Jorgia knowing all this stuff about me and my family. But I still felt uneasy that people who didn't even really know me or care about me—people like Jorgia's sister— had witnessed something as personal and sensitive as my Mom losing it. It made me feel very vulnerable.

I braced myself for how Jorgia's sister would react when she recognized me. We locked eyes for a brief moment but, without a word, she strapped herself in and sat there without eating her snack.

"I've been telling your Ate Jacq here the same but does she listen?" Jorgia's mom droned on as the car engine purred to life and we drove past the school gates. "You are young, talented, intelligent women! Why waste your energy running after boys when you can change the world?"

"Daddy says you used to stalk him in Chem lab," Jorgia rebutted.

"Don't listen to a thing your Dad tells you, that fool. Except when he's right, of course. But he isn't now. I was never boy-_ _ _ _ _ like that."

"Turn right here please, Tita," I said, pointing at the corner of the block. Jorgia's mom steered the car to the right.

"We're not chasing after boys," Jorgia answered. "Cayt can't even string five words together in front of him."

"Hey! That's not public info," I hissed.

"*You* said you had a crush first!" Jorgia hissed back.

"Is that true, Cayt? Don't be shy! Just be yourself and they'll see how amazing you are."

"So what is it really? Do we run or hide or what?" Jorgia countered.

"Oh just do your homework before you think about boys or TikTok or whatever you kids are obsessed with these days. That's my rule. What's your Mom's rule about boys, Cayt?"

"Oh uhm . . ." I stammered. I couldn't remember the last time Mom sat me down for a talk but I was pretty sure I could've cared less about boys then. Not that I did care now. I think.

"Have you ever heard of the words 'verbal filter?' Stop grilling us already, Ma, and we promise not to date until we get our senior citizen cards."

"That's our house there," I said, pointing at Elvira.

"Don't be silly, Jorg. Thirty-five is a perfectly reasonable age to start dating."

I started to chuckle but Jorgia cut me off.

"Don't laugh just to be polite, Cayt. She'll think she's actually funny."

"Ouch! Below the belt, daughter," Jorgia's mom said just as she steered the car to a halt in front of our apartment. She turned to me and said, "Sure you don't wanna go to Paradiso with us, Cayt?"

"Oh, I'm sure that I want to," I answered as I prepared to scoot out of the car. "It's just that I can't. My Dad has to leave for a business emergency so I gotta be with my Mom and Sam."

"Oh no. Not too bad of an emergency, I hope? But I'm sure your mom and sister can survive a few hours without you. You want me to go ask her for permission?"

"Oh… uhm…" My mind raced in search of a good excuse. How could I tell Jorgia's mom that, no, contrary to what other people might think or expect, Mom could not be left alone with my sister? Sure, she had been a bit more active the last couple of weeks—but maybe too active? And yet she never actually got anything done right. Losing my permission slip was just one on a very long list of attempts on Mom's part to be parent-like again.

I looked desperately at Jorgia who, without knowing my exact thoughts, knew exactly what help I needed.

"Mom! We can take her some other time. Stop being so pushy," Jorgia said, rolling her eyes at her mom for dramatic effect. Then, she winked at me.

"Thanks," I whispered to Jorgia before climbing out of their car and waving them off.

It was half past seven in the evening and Dad would miss his bus to Cauayan if he didn't stop pestering us about all the things we needed to do while he was away for two days.

"Dad! You do know that you could just call us if you forgot something, right? Though I doubt if you did," I said, holding up three pages of instructions in Dad's tiny handwriting. Over the past weeks, Dad and I had semi-fallen back into our usual banter. I think we both wanted to set aside our previous disagreement and not bringing it up was how we chose to do it.

"I know, I know. Oh! I forgot to mention. I asked the landlady to check on you while I'm gone too, okay? Invite Mrs. Suaco for lunch," Dad said as he swept the room with his eyes and felt his pockets. Then he sighed. "I hate having to leave you but I really need to go."

"Stop being so jittery and go already," Mom said, carrying Dad's bulging overnight bag to the front door. "Sam and I squeezed in a few crossword books there in case you get bored."

"Thanks, hun, but I probably only need one," Dad said as he unzipped his bag and unloaded half a dozen of the little books and gave them for Sam to hold. "I can't wait to get some shut-eye."

"Alright, well let's go before you miss your bus! The girls and I will drive you," Mom said, taking the keys from behind the door and making her way out of the house.

"No!" Dad called out after her. "I mean, no *need*. You girls rest. I've booked a car, see?"

"But it's so early! We're not tired yet, are we, girls?"

I noticed Dad fidget with the handles of his bag. He probably didn't want Mom to drive. Come to think of it, I don't remember Mom having been behind the wheel even once since she gave birth to Miggy. I could understand if Dad was apprehensive about letting her drive, especially here in Manila. If Mom lost her cool over spilled rice, I was afraid to find out what she'd do if somebody cut in front of us or rammed our car or something.

Just then, there was a ding on Dad's phone. We looked up and saw an orange sedan slow down to a halt right in front of our apartment. Dad's face broke into such a huge grin, you'd have thought the car was his to keep.

"There's my ride! Can't cancel it now, Anna. I'd still have to pay for it," he said, turning to me and Sam. "Alright, give Dad a kiss."

Sam wrapped her tiny limbs around Dad in a bear hug. Then Mom gave Dad a kiss on the lips, lingering longer than usual, and for the briefest moment, I saw in my head something similar happening between me and a certain wavy-haired boy.

Finally, Dad approached me. I gave him a quick peck on his cheeks and made to move away, eager to shake off any kissing images from my head. But Dad held on to me and whispered, "Watch over them, Cayt. I'm counting on you."

With a final wave, Dad slipped on his face mask and got into the car, which quickly rode off into the distance.

I held Sam by the shoulders and steered her towards our front door as she started singing that song about dreams from *The Greatest Showman*. We were almost inside when I heard, between the chorus lines, the familiar beep that told me that our SUV had been unlocked. I turned around to see Mom opening the car on the driver's side, her eyes twinkling in the dark.

"I just realized. I don't remember the last time we went to the mall. Do you?"

Sam stopped squawking. I tightened my grip on her shoulders as we looked at each other. I guess we were both thinking the same thing: how could we forget the last time we were at the mall with Mom?

Sam inched closer to me and started twisting the hem of my shirt. I ran my hand across her back to try to reassure her.

"It's late, Mom," I called at her from the safety of our front door. "Let's go when Dad comes back."

"No! Let's go now! We can still go shopping and catch a movie after," Mom said, a big smile on her face. But it wasn't scary like a clown. It seemed kinda inviting, actually. Like she was really excited to take us out.

I looked at Sam, her eyes wide and round.

"Do you wanna go?" I asked. After a moment's hesitation, Sam shook her head slowly. I nodded at her.

"We don't wanna go, Mom. Please, can we just stay at home? Let's watch a movie here."

I watched as Mom closed the car door and walked towards us. She squatted on the floor so that her face was just a few inches away from Sam's. She looked at us as she spoke.

"Don't you wanna have a fun night with Mom? Hmm?"

I drew a sharp breath. I did miss having fun with Mom. So much. But it wasn't possible anymore, was it? I didn't say a word—and neither did Sam.

"I know I've lost my temper at you girls for no reason before. And I'm really sorry…You know I'm sorry, right?" Mom looked at us, a pleading in her eyes and in the way her hands clung tightly onto both me and Sam. "You know I love you, right?"

Since Miggy died, Mom was uncontrollably sad or angry a lot of times. Dad said it was because she loved him so much and she couldn't bear having lost him. I wanted to think that she loved us in the same way too.

I gave the slightest of nods.

With tears welling in her eyes, Mom smiled and hugged us tightly. When she let go, she looked at us again with a big grin and said, "Now will you let Mom make it up to you by taking you out to the mall?

Sam and I looked at each other again. I bet she was just as eager as I was to let Mom get started on making up for the last year and a half. We nodded and, after cheers of victory on Mom's part, I grabbed our things, checked that we hadn't left anything plugged in or charging inside the house, and locked our front door. Then we climbed into our vehicle and let Mom drive us to the mall.

While we did steer clear of that Korean grill, we pretty much hit every other place in Fisher. Mom must've felt really sorry for how she had behaved in the past months because she filled our grocery cart with all of my and Sam's favorite potato chips and candy bars, most of which Dad would usually only let us buy in small quantities and when they were half off and a week shy of expiring. At the toy store, Mom didn't flinch when Sam asked her to get her a teepee *and* a mermaid tail. Where Sam was ever gonna use that mermaid tail puzzled me but I couldn't help but feel excited over the teepee too.

I thought that was the end of our night out and really didn't expect anything more but Mom insisted on going inside the gadget store after seeing me fawn over a set of red speakers that even I had to admit were absurdly overpriced. But I guess Mom was acting a little absurd because she did buy it for me, all while chatting nonstop and acting weirdly chummy with the sales dude (they were fist-bumping with each other by closing time).

I couldn't believe that we had an incident-free night at the mall *and* got to buy all of the stuff we wanted. But the best thing about it all was that I felt that Mom cared for us again. Not just because she bought us stuff (which even normal Mom hardly ever did) but because she remembered what we liked and paid attention to us, asking about school and our friends the way she always used to before.

For the first time in almost two years, I felt really close to my Mom again.

I liked feeling that way a lot.

NO RETURN, NO EXCHANGE

To get a pretty good day with Mom these days was a miracle. To get two was impossible—or so I had thought until that weekend. As it turns out, I needn't have worried so much about Dad being away because Mom seemed like normal happy Mom again, only kinda better actually.

Sure, she was a mess at chores (I guess that was what you got when you're out of practice then try to cook lunch, do the laundry, and mop the floors all at the same time). But at least she was cool about doing it all herself and wasn't even nagging us to help. Then she stayed up with me and Sam inside the new teepee on Friday and Saturday nights, while we binged on animated films and all the junk we had bought at the mall. Ironically, Mom was so fun that I was the one who had to remind her on Sunday afternoon that Sam and I had homework. It was so weird to have to turn Mom away when she came crashing into our room, begging us to let her experiment on our hair with washable hair color markers.

That night, once all our worksheets were done, we cuddled in our parents' bed next to each other, all three of us, as Mom reenacted scenes from her stint as a production assistant for a film company. I had been so focused on comparing how our Mom had been the past year to the Mom I knew before Miggy died—but I never really thought much of the woman she had been before she was a mom at all.

Sam had fallen asleep, but I couldn't get enough of Mom being with us right now, so I fiddled with my camera settings in an effort to stay awake and filmed the two of them while they lay on the bed.

Did she ever regret marrying Dad, having kids, quitting her job, and moving to Cauayan? I asked without thinking.

Mom paused for dramatic effect. Immediately, I wished I hadn't asked her. What if I didn't like the answer? I pretended to be particularly interested in recording the ceiling.

"You were barely three years old when we wrapped up filming for this really funny zombie movie," Mom said wistfully.

"I have a lot of regrets in life… Not having a real relationship with my parents, for instance. Letting other people make decisions for me, especially when I was younger… getting worked up about what everyone else thought about me. I guess I am sorry that I had to choose… or *felt* that I had to choose at the time. I would've liked to have done both, you know? And looking back, I think maybe I could have. Wait, what am I saying? Of course I could have!" Mom said, flexing her biceps. "But if you're asking if I regret choosing you over all of that…"

I braced myself for what she would say next. Mom took my phone from me and checked to see that it was still recording. Then she held it up to her face, beaming.

"I do *not* regret it," she said with emphasis. "Not one bit!"

As Mom pressed her forehead against mine, I looked into her eyes feeling quite certain that this day was about to become one of my favorites.

I woke up early the next morning feeling like somebody had shoved ice underneath my blanket. As I sat up and threw back the covers, I looked down and, true enough, there was an ice cube melting on my lap.

I looked up, puzzled, and saw Mom doing the same thing to Sam.

"Get up, sleepyheads! It's time for another adventure!"

"Come on," Mom chirped, lifting Sam up over her shoulders and disappearing into the master bathroom with her. I heard the shower come on, and a tiny shriek from Sam, probably because the water heater had yet to warm up. After a minute, Mom emerged from the bathroom, a big grin plastered on her face as she looked at me. "Get ready, we're going to the park!"

"Mom, what—?" I replied as I grabbed my phone to check the time. It was a whole three hours before my alarm was scheduled to go off. "It's a school day."

"School pfft! What could you miss in a day?"

I squinted at Mom. Then I looked around for Dad. This had to be a test, right?

"Come on, get up or we'll miss the sunrise!"

"I'd rather miss that over school," I was surprised to find myself saying. When did I become *this* responsible?

"Okay, fine!" Mom said as she tugged at the covers again. "We'll just drop by for an hour so you can get to school on time. Happy?"

I was not happy. I was very sleepy. Mom didn't let us go to bed until midnight and I've only had four hours of sleep since. But I guess I should be thankful it was happy Mom who was keeping us up rather than angry zombie Mom, right?

I stared at Mom's puppy dog eyes and felt my reluctance ebbing away.

"One hour," I said sternly.

Mom was cheering and doing high kicks before I had even rolled off the bed.

In just thirty minutes, Mom had us buckled up in the car on our way to Rizal Park. When we arrived, there were already a bunch of people jogging or cycling or walking their dogs there even if it was only five o'clock in the morning. We skipped around the huge musical fountain (which absolutely delighted Sam), took wacky photos at the Japanese Garden, and even saw the changing of guards at the monument.

It was not at all a bad way to spend the morning. But before we knew it, more than an hour had passed and we had to make a mad dash for our school things.

Mom weaved in and out of traffic, leaving more than a few cars honking at us from behind. When our car finally skidded to a halt at the curb in front of our apartment, we shot out of our seats and ran towards the front door where Dad was waiting for us.

"WHERE HAVE YOU BEEN?!" Dad demanded, his face red.

Mom, Sam, and I froze in our tracks.

The vein on Dad's temple was throbbing furiously. I had never seen him like this before.

"Look at the time!" Dad continued. "No message. The house looks like it's been ransacked! All of you and the car—GONE!"

Nobody spoke or even moved. The silence was only broken when Dad's watch chimed to mark a new hour, reminding me that we had a flag ceremony to catch.

"Dad," I finally squeaked. "Sorry but… we need to get our things or we'll be late for school."

"Well you should've thought about that earlier!" Dad scolded me.

I couldn't answer and looked down at the floor instead. Dad spoke again but, this time, his voice sounded a little more restrained.

"Fine. Girls, get dressed and be back in five."

Sam and I bolted for the stairs before Dad could even finish his sentence.

Inside our room, I tore through our closet and grabbed a dress for Sam before wiggling into my own uniform. Then I started tossing our school things into our bags only to realize that I had left a couple of notebooks in our parents' room. I hollered at Sam to hurry up then proceeded to run downstairs to get them. But I stopped when I saw Mom and Dad standing across each other in the living room, talking in raised voices.

"Well, I *should* have a say! I am as much their parent as you are," Mom was saying.

"You drove without a license, Anna! And let's not forget the fact that you've been mentally unstable—"

"—I am not!" Mom yelled, covering her ears as she spoke.

"—for the past months. You could've gotten yourselves killed!" Dad exploded. "Does that sound like something a parent in their *right* mind would do?!"

"Why do you always think the worst of me? I got us all back in one piece, didn't I? You just hate that I'm the cool parent now."

"What am I, twelve? There is nothing cool about endangering our girls and setting a bad example for them. You're acting like a kid, Anna."

"You're acting like a kid, Anna," Mom repeated in a high-pitched voice.

"Real mature. You know what? Keep doing that. I'm going to take the girls to school and be the parent for both of us."

Mom kept mimicking and pulling faces as she disappeared into their bedroom.

Finally, Dad turned in the direction of the stairs, where Sam had joined me midway through our parents' fighting.

"Don't just stand there. Let's go," Dad said, motioning for us to follow him outside.

We scuttled after him and climbed silently into the car. The moment I shut the door behind me, Dad spoke.

"I told you to take care of things while I was gone, Cayt. I expected more from you."

Me? I thought, my stomach dropping. Was this my fault?

I wanted to ask or say something. But I couldn't. Not when Dad looked so disappointed at me. Without waiting for me to answer, he started the engine and drove us to school without another word.

I hated that I had let Dad down. Just when we were starting to be on good terms again, too.

I was so bothered that Law had to throw a rubber eraser at me to realize that Mrs. Aguirre had called my name during roll twice already. After homeroom, she asked me to help carry her books to the faculty room. As we walked down the hallway and passed by the juniors' classrooms, I found my neck involuntarily craning to see if a certain wavy-haired boy would be inside one of them.

"You seem to be quite distracted this morning, Cayt," Mrs. Aguirre said out of the blue.

"Oh, was I?" I said, rolling back my shoulders so that I stood at attention. "I guess I'm just tired. I didn't get much sleep."

"Looks like you had an exciting weekend," Mrs. Aguirre said, her voice gentle.

"I guess you could say that," I answered, trying to keep my tone upbeat.

Just then, we caught up to Sir Li, who was balancing a couple of gigantic and funny-looking projects in his arms. "Hi George. Need a hand?"

"No, I got it. Thanks, Jaymee. Oh, hi Cayt!"

"Good morning, Sir," I answered, picking up a huge styrofoam block that had toppled from the pile Sir Li was carrying.

"Did you get the link for practice sheets that I sent you?" He asked as he let me place the block on top of the other models.

"I started on them last week," I answered. Though I wasn't able to do much during the weekend on account of our slumber party with Mom.

"Okay, great! Now excuse me, I have to dump these on my desk so I can grade them before I accidentally ruin them all."

I watched as Sir Li skidded off into the faculty room.

"You know, Cayt, some experts have said that distractedness could be a sign of anxiety," Mrs. Aguirre said once Sir Li had gone. "It would be understandable if you were feeling some pressure with school..."

I nodded silently, considering Mrs. Aguirre's statement.

"I'm here anytime you need somebody to talk to, okay?" Mrs. Aguirre said, her eyes smiling. "We can deal with our stress together."

"You get stressed out, too?" I asked, a bit surprised. Mrs. Aguirre always seemed so cool.

"Of course, I think everybody does. We *all* need help from time to time. When that time comes, know that I'm here for you."

It was one thing to talk with friends about the things that bothered you and another entirely to discuss it with a teacher. Were things really bad enough to merit that? And if I talked with her, would the other kids know? Would it go on my school record? How would that look like in future applications?

"Okay, I'll remember that. Thanks," I said to Mrs. Aguirre before trudging back to our classroom for the next period.

After school, Dad picked me and Sam up and dropped us off at home so he could run errands at the mall. Sam went straight upstairs while I went to the kitchen to grab a snack. I hadn't even finished pouring myself a glass of milk when I heard a loud wail come from our bedroom upstairs.

"What the—?" I said, accidentally spilling some milk on the table. I hastened out of the kitchen and bumped into Mom, who was running out of their bedroom.

"Oh no, she found out," Mom said, looking frantic.

"What are you talking about?" I asked. Just then, I heard the distinct sound of Sam's small feet banging heavily on the floor.

"Your Dad is returning all the stuff we bought," Mom explained. "The teepee, everything. He said we couldn't afford it."

I listened as, upstairs, Sam continued to throw a tantrum. Neither Mom nor I made a move to stop her. I guess we both felt she deserved the freedom to be upset.

Mom sat on the couch and I followed suit. After a few moments of silence, Mom spoke again.

"Your Dad said he couldn't believe how I had acted… But Cayt," Mom continued, "I'm not doing these things on purpose. I can't explain it. I don't understand what's going on inside me."

I bit my lip. A huge part of me couldn't figure Mom out either.

I looked into Mom's eyes even though I was afraid of what I might see. They were dark, black, bottomless pools. She covered them with her palms as she started trembling.

"I don't know what I'm going to do, Cayt," Mom said, her voice muffled by her sobs. "I can't help what I feel or think or even do sometimes."

I stared at my feet as I listened to Mom.

"I want to be happy, I know that I should be but… I'm just not," Mom continued. "I don't know why it affects me this way, Cayt… Am I just weak?"

I couldn't speak. I wouldn't. For almost a year, nobody had ever talked about what was happening. Mom had never told me how she really felt. But now that I sort of knew, I had no idea what difference knowing actually made.

"Sometimes I feel you and Sam and Dad would be better off without me here, you know?"

I gave in to the urge to hug Mom and whispered to her, "That's not true," sure that it was the right thing to say.

If I had wondered about it before—about the possibility of living away from Mom—then I guess it was silly to think she hadn't thought of it either. She knew and Dad knew and I knew and maybe even Sam knew that, most of the time, she was an extra person to either look after and even be wary of.

"I don't know what I'd do if I turned into such a burden for you and your dad. I think I'd rather just not… be here."

Mom held on to my hands as she said this, so I managed to look into her eyes again. But they were empty. I felt a chill run up my spine.

Somehow I sensed that Mom wasn't simply talking about running away to live on a sunny El Nido beach. I couldn't shake off the feeling that she was on the verge of doing something unthinkable again. And I was deeply disturbed by the possibility that, this time, it could end up being irreversible.

In the days that followed, I had been running downstairs to my parents' room the moment I woke up, just to check that Mom was still there and hadn't packed her bags—or worse.

Most days I'd catch her reading in bed. Some days, their bed would be empty and my heart would skip two beats. But then I'd hear small noises in the kitchen and would feel reassured that, if Mom had gone, I wouldn't be hearing something as normal as a kettle whistling.

On Friday, I tiptoed outside their room and opened their door by a crack, same as I had been doing the last three days when—

"Gotcha!"

I jumped at the sound of Dad's voice from behind my ear.

"Aargh! You're so immature," I said, rolling my eyes as Dad laughed at his own prank. He had returned to his good-natured ways just a couple of days after his row with Mom.

"Wooh!" Dad finally said, once he had contained his laughter. "Cayt, let me tell you. It was worth all the trouble raising you just to see that look on your face."

"Ha-ha. Glad to know you had no regrets having me," I said as I punched Dad's arm. It was the first light moment we shared since Monday.

"So why have you been sneaking into our room every morning without so much as a glance at my wallet?" Dad asked.

"Like you would leave your wallet behind."

"So you have been looking for it!"

"Puh-lease! I've known not to bother since third grade. You don't keep that many bills."

"Can't be too careful with you girls around," Dad said.

We fell silent and I had a pretty good inkling we were both remembering our last mishap involving money (among other things). Dad switched gears and broke the ice.

"So why *have* you been checking on our room the past days?"

I looked at Dad. He was smiling but his eyes didn't quite turn down like a rainbow the way ours were supposed to when we were actually happy. I bet he was still recovering from the row with Mom. And the business—I didn't have any idea how bad it was but it must've been if he had risked leaving Mom and me and Cayt alone, with only an aging landlady next-door to come to our aid.

I didn't want to add to Dad's troubles. I mean, look at that groove between his eyebrows. Was it just me or had it been etched in there overnight? Despite the CD collection Dad refused to get rid of and his many eighties references, I had never seen him as old until now.

"No reason," I stammered as I turned on my heels. "*Byegottagetreadyforschool!*"

"Hold it!" Dad said, holding on to my arm. "What are you not telling me, Cayt?"

"What're you talking about?" I feigned.

"Is it about Mom?" Dad whispered. He was holding both my arms now and looking straight into my eyes with his laser vision. Shoot.

"If it is, you need to tell me, Cayt. Remember, we're taking care of Mom together, right?"

I nodded and opened my mouth, then hesitated. Mom said she didn't want to be a burden to Dad. Would this count?

"Cayt, don't even think about it. Just tell me exactly what you know."

I looked up at Dad. Who was I gonna listen to—him or Mom? Was there even a dilemma here? Of course I should tell the responsible adult, right?

"Dad, you have to promise not to freak. It's just that I think…" I whispered, checking around me for a sign of Mom. The coast was clear.

"I think Mom wants to kill herself."

I regretted my decision the moment I saw Dad's face crumple, as if all his dreams had come crashing down at his feet.

I shoved my notebooks into my bag as soon as the last bell rang and got on my feet, saying a hurried goodbye to Law and Jorg.

"Hello? Earth to Cayt?! We have film club, remember?" Jorgia said, scratching on an invisible turntable in the air.

Oh shoot. We were supposed to help build the booth after school today.

"Now she remembers. Where has your head been these days?" Jorgia asked as we walked out of our classroom, towards the basement canteen.

"Ugh. I'd like to know, same as you. But I'm not going to club today."

"Why the heck not?" Jorgia demanded. Wiggling her eyebrows, she added, "Noel's gonna be there for sure this time."

"I DON'T CARE, OKAY?" I shouted, raising my voice without even realizing. "I'M NOT GOING!"

"Sheesh! Alright, alright," Jorgia said, hands up in the air. "Don't go all Hulk-ish on me—"

"—Don't pressure me then," I retorted.

"Sorry, I just wanted to hang out," Jorgia said, her voice soft. "If you don't want to then no big deal."

"Look, I'm sorry, Jorg," I said apologetically, taking a deep breath and forcing myself to calm down. Was I turning into a zombie like Mom too? "It's just that, things have been… tricky at home. I just can't go to club right now because there's so much to do," I tried to explain.

"I was wondering why you haven't been posting any boring good morning stories lately—"

"Boring?!" I squealed. "Why do you reply with cry-laughing emojis then?"

"Uh, 'coz we're friends and I support you? Duh. Doesn't mean you're a comedic genius."

"That really hurts, you know."

"Yeah well, friends tell the truth, even when it hurts. Like, you wouldn't let me go in front of everyone without telling me I had food stuck in my teeth, would you?"

I paused for a moment, recalling how I had let such a situation take place just a few days ago at the caf.

"So, what's going on?" Jorgia asked, seriously this time. "Is it your mom?"

I nodded lightly, unsure if I was really willing to confirm it with Jorgia.

"You can tell me if you want."

I nodded again and looked at Jorgia. There was something in the way her brows furrowed that made it seem like, without knowing what they were, she had already taken on my problems as hers.

I dragged Jorgia to a deserted corner by a stairway and told her everything. About the pills and the bath tub. The cactus. The bowl of rice. The shopping spree. The impromptu field trip, and the shouting match with Dad. I told her about what Mom had confessed to me a week ago. How I had been checking on her in the mornings. And now, Dad. How I had been watching him from my bedroom window, chain-smoking outside the house in the middle of the night, every night that had passed since he found out about Mom. How he had signed me and Sam up for the school bus service so Mom would never be out of his sight. How he wore the same shirt days in a row and how I had the stinking suspicion that he sometimes forgot to take a shower or brush his teeth because he was so preoccupied with us and Mom and work and the house and Mom.

Jorgia and I looked at each other grimly after I had finished unloading all of this on her. Without a word, she unclasped one of her hands from mine, just long enough to hand me a crumpled tissue from her bag.

PAST, INHERITED

In Science class, our teacher warned us that we would either become our worst nightmares—or become in-laws with them.

After a brief introduction to genetics (Gregor Mendel was a friar *and* a scientist!), our teacher had us exchange photos of our moms and dads with our seat mates. We were supposed to take turns identifying which traits the other inherited from either of their parents. I had already finished Law's and now, he had zoomed in on my parents' wedding photo on my tablet and was holding it up to my face, sliding it up and down to bring it to level with whatever facial feature he was comparing at the moment.

"Nose is fifty-fifty... But you have your Mom's eyes and eyebrows. And ears! Hmm... you're so alike," Law added as he wrote it down on the activity sheet.

"Are you blind? I am *not* like my Mom at all," I argued. "We're like coffee and milk!"

"Skin tone is just one trait. Look," Law said, double-tapping at Mom's face. "It's undeniable, Cayt."

"Listen: I'm more like my Dad, okay? You better get it right or we'll fail the assignment."

"This isn't graded! And there's something very wrong with you if you'd rather look like your Dad. No offense to the man but he's only half as good-looking as your Mom."

"There is nothing wrong with me! Gimme that," I said, snatching the sheet from Law.

"Yeah, yeah," I heard him mutter underneath his breath. "Girls."

Forget genetics, I thought as I blanketed our paper with correction tape. I was not going to become what I feared the most, if I had any say in the matter.

When Sam and I got home after school that day, we walked in on Dad in the kitchen, chopping potatoes. Sam plopped down on a chair and dove into a can of cheese corn balls immediately, while I tossed my bag on the table and sidled up to the stove, lifting the lid of the pot to catch a whiff of what was stewing inside.

Adobo. Again.

We've been eating pretty much every variation of the dish in the past week. There was the regular kind that was meat braised in soy sauce and vinegar. Then there were the other varieties: dried up, with coconut milk, white (no soy sauce), with bananas, with eggs. And now, with potatoes. I sure was starting to miss Ate Fe and Lola.

"Shoot!" I heard Dad hiss underneath his breath. He hopped to the sink and put his finger under running water. I peered at his hand and saw little beads of blood trickling out from between the raw pink flesh where he had cut himself. Almost instinctively, I put my face as close as possible to Dad's hand to study how real blood looked. I've used ketchup, tomato sauce, poster paint with cornstarch, and the fake blood from film club, but I had yet to be satisfied with the consistency of any of those.

Dad wrestled me away from his hands. "You're weird, kid."

"Well who raised me?" I retorted before saying, "I'll get the Betadine."

I walked past Sam, whose lips and paws were now a bright orange, and tiptoed into my parents' room, where Mom seemed to have been hypnotized by the home shopping channel. After a quick and probably unnoticed "hi," I made a beeline for the medicine cabinet in their bathroom and found the first aid kit behind the boxes and bottles of pain reliever and anti-allergy and anti-diarrhea pills.

I returned to the kitchen, where Dad was already back at the chopping board, his left hand wrapped in a kitchen towel. He seemed to be struggling with the chore but, interestingly enough, not because of his injury.

"Isn't that knife too small?" I asked as he held out his sliced finger for me to clean and cover with a band-aid.

"Hmm?" Dad murmured, looking surprised that I had noticed. "Oh. I was too lazy to get a bigger one."

I tutted at him and asked, "Is that the example you wanna set for your two daughters?" Then I turned around to grab a knife from the block on the counter—only there were none.

"Uhm. Did someone break into our house and steal all our other knives?"

"Ha ha," Dad said, wiping his hands on the towel and walking towards the sink.

I watched as Dad opened the cupboard underneath and pulled out half a dozen boxes before finally excavating a shoebox that had been wrapped tightly in rope. He tugged and twisted at the knots gingerly, careful not to put any strain on his injured finger, before he managed to untie them completely. Then he lifted the lid to reveal a magpie collection of all our kitchen knives, a couple of steak knives I had never seen before, and even an ice pick.

I raised an eyebrow at him. "Really?"

Dad shrugged as he took a slightly larger knife (but still not the best one for really fast chopping the way Ate Fe does it) and began redoing the knots.

"Is this how it's gonna be from now on?" I asked as he stashed the boxes back inside the cupboard.

Dad gave me a half smile, the kind that wasn't really happy but just smiled for the sake of smiling.

"Only until things get better, Cayt."

Dad got up on his feet and went back to preparing dinner, while I crawled all the way up to my room, deep in thought.

Could things get better?

And if they couldn't, was I really destined to become like Mom?

The truth was we did look alike. And before Miggy, we liked doing so many of the same things—usually together—and I used to be proud of the fact. Mom was the reason I loved film so much, something about myself that I've always liked. But now I worried that I would inherit her _ _ _ _ _ too.

In twenty years, would I be drawing the curtains shut every morning and refusing to get out of bed until the sun had melted into an orange haze? Would I shun everybody around me and leave my family to fend for themselves while I hid in the dark like a fearsome monster? Would I, on the rare occasions I emerged from hiding, encourage my young ones to act recklessly, without any concern for how my actions could affect my family in the long run? And would I tell my fourteen-year-old daughter that I sometimes wished I could disappear from the world—to stop existing, if only to stop hurting?

It didn't seem like much of a future at all. It was definitely not what I wanted for myself. So, for the next few days, I made a conscious effort to act as unlike Mom as I could.

Get up early and do all my chores without Dad making me? Check.

Smile and say "good morning" to everyone—from the ushers at church to the cashiers at the canteen? Check.

Be super optimistic and only watch movies with happy endings? Check and check.

Refrain from biting Sam's head off when she loses my one pastel highlighter? ~~Check~~.

Well, nobody's perfect. But I figured I was still doing alright. It was definitely easier to be normal and happy at school though (where pointy objects need not be excessively safeguarded), which was why I grabbed any opportunity to stay there longer. The past weeks, I had missed a lot of film club meets on account of the fact that I had chores to do at home and had to take turns with Dad keeping an eye on Mom. But with the school fair *and* midterms fast approaching, I felt like I was within my rights to take a break and be a normal kid for a day.

On Wednesday, I joined the last film club meeting before the fair. Jorgia and I dragged Law with us since he didn't belong to any club and could therefore be let in on our plans for world domination (which could not be said of either Alex or Hallie, who belonged to the dance squad).

The three of us were assigned to organize question cards for our booth's main guest players. Law's expansive knowledge about the school and the students and faculty—while surprising for somebody who usually spent lunch breaks in the classroom—came in handy when tweaking the questions.

"So, Mrs. Aguirre's an alumni too?" I confirmed with Law before editing the form on my tablet. "Alright, here's the question for Mrs. Castro: 'Mrs. Aguirre, Ms. Katigbak, Mr. Li, and Brother Franz were still studying at Lorenzo High when you first assumed your post as a Disciplinary Officer. Rank them from best to worst in terms of their disciplinary records.'"

We broke into laughter at the thought of Mrs. Castro being forced to slurp Soup No. Five rather than jeopardize the reputation of our faculty.

"Oh man," Jorgia wheezed in between giggles. "I cannot wait for Sunday!"

"Aren't you nervous about the questions you'll be asked during your turn?" Law asked.

"Nah. Cayt and I are playing against Sir Li. I bet we'll get generic questions."

"'Have you ever cheated on a test?' is a generic question," Law argued.

"Well I don't need to answer anything because my gut is made of steel," Jorgia said, pointing at her belly.

"Truth," I agreed, remembering how gamely Jorgia tried Dad's *pinapaitan* when she came over one weekend.

Just then, Noel dropped by at our table. "Done with the questions?"

I nodded wordlessly while Jorgia updated the file on the Cloud. As she did, Noel sat beside me and, nodding towards Law, whispered, "Who's the kid?"

"Oh, uh… he's our friend," I stammered, the hairs on my neck standing up. "His name's Law. But he's not in any other club, don't worry."

"Okay, just checking," Noel said, straightening up. Then, so Jorg and Law could hear, he said, "We're playing a movie after. Feel free to stick around."

"That's okay," Law started to say, "we still need to do our Bio—OW!"

Jorg and I had kicked him in the shin at the same time, apparently.

"We'll stay," Jorgia said, absolutely beaming.

Fifteen minutes later, the three of us were spread out on the floor of the AV room, watching Swarog's *Mana* with the rest of the club.

The movie was about a family matriarch who passed away, leaving her five adult children to go on a sort of scavenger hunt inside the ancestral home as a way of earning their inheritance. As the film progressed, it became pretty clear that wealth wasn't the only thing that the mother had passed down to her children—but a dangerous, violent streak as well.

Some scenes had us screaming so loud and in unison that a school custodian barged into the room to check what the commotion was all about. After Noel cleared the matter, we continued watching in horror as the siblings in the movie literally tore each other apart.

"Her kids don't stand a chance," I heard Noel whisper to someone from somewhere behind me. "*Psycho*, *Hereditary*. Isn't that what they're all trying to say? We're bound to repeat our parents' mistakes."

Jorgia turned around to shush Noel, saying, "Give Swarog some credit."

A couple of kids in front of us nodded in agreement.

We watched the remainder of the movie in peace (sort of) until the end, when one of the kids managed to get out alive by giving up her inheritance and using the combat skills she had mastered inside to rebuild her life from scratch.

"What does it mean, though?" Law asked, scratching his head as the three of us walked to Profanitea after film club.

"That, contrary to what Noel and some other movies have said," Jorgia started, "we do *not* have to inherit our parents' crap?"

"Okaaay. But she did inherit the combat skills," Law argued.

"True…" Jorgia said, nodding slowly. "Maybe it means you can choose what you inherit?" The sword-fighting skills are cool. But seriously, I don't get why they even fought over that house. It was so old-fashioned!"

"*That's* why you wouldn't want it?" Law chortled. "I was more bothered by the torture chamber in the basement."

We made our way inside the milk tea place and headed for our favorite table by an open window, where Jorgia and Law continued to rattle off all the things they didn't like about the house in the movie. But I was still trying to answer Law's first question.

When the main character had escaped, the movie could've already ended. But it went on for another five minutes to show the protagonist leaving her old desk job and finding success in wielding swords and throwing knives for a living. It mirrored the opening scene, when she was being taught to do the same as a child, though for a more sinister purpose.

She didn't choose to have the skillset of an assassin. In fact, she had tried to leave that life behind before, without much luck. It was only when she confronted and eventually accepted her past that she found the courage to literally brandish it as a weapon and carve a better future for herself.

Genetics may determine who I am. But it doesn't get to choose who I become.

I do.

FAIR MANIA

I walked onto the Lorenzo open field on Sunday feeling invincible.

Everywhere around me, Lorenzo High kids buzzed with excitement as they darted aggressively from one attraction to another in what was, undeniably, fair mania. And it was contagious. Within fifteen minutes, Jorgia and I had already parted with most of our money in exchange for milkshakes and churros and temporary tattoos.

"Where is he?!" Jorgia asked as she gnawed on her last churro. "I wanna go on the inflatables before the lines get really long."

"No idea," I said in between sips of my milkshake. "He hasn't seen my messages."

"Of all the days! This is *so* not like him."

Just then, I caught sight of Law running towards us. He looked extra sporty in sneakers and red track pants that matched his face mask.

"What are you wearing?" I asked him curiously.

"Finally!" Jorgia said at the same time.

"Sorry!" Law said, panting. "I can explain."

"Don't explain, just make up for it by taking us to the inflatables!" Jorgia insisted. Law and I let her drag us to the two-storey inflatable castle, where we jumped around like rabid toddlers until we were out of breath. At one point, I was worried that the ube milkshake I had just downed would come back up but, thankfully, it didn't.

The three of us hit a few more stalls and attractions but mostly to just look around, now that we were running low on cash. We laughed at the state of the rickety coaster that had been installed in the middle of the lawn, wondering if they had been renting it ever since Lorenzo was founded in 1945. We held our breaths and dashed past the kiosk selling flavored curly fries so we wouldn't be tempted. Finally, we walked to the side of the field where the club booths were all clustered and saw Hallie and Alex waving at us to come over.

As we drew nearer, I noticed that the two girls were wearing the exact same red track pants that Law had on. I looked at Law beside me; Jorgia was staring at him too, looking dumbstruck.

"Surprise!" Law said, beaming.

I jumped up and down then hugged Law. "When did this happen?! *How* did this happen?"

"We were just as shocked as you are," Alex said as she came up to us.

"Explain yourself, young man!" Jorgia demanded, mimicking Mrs. Castro. We laughed.

"I dunno," Law said, shrugging his shoulders, "after that film club meeting, something just… pushed me to do it."

"Wow… film must really suck then," Alex teased. We laughed some more.

We stuck around to cheer Law, Alex, and Hallie on as they performed a short routine along with a few other dance club members. Law was such a natural, it was almost unnerving. Afterwards, Jorgia and I parted with our precious pesos to support their trampoline and velcro booth. As it turned out, I had a pretty high jump. Law and Alex strained themselves a bit trying to unstick me from the wall. Once they had finally gotten me down, Jorg and I made a run for our own booth since we were supposed to have reported for duty two minutes ago.

The film club booth was located by the flagpole. Jorgia and I excitedly elbowed our way past the small crowd that had gathered in front of it. Noel was at the front, gleefully collecting money from bystanders as they voted for whom they wanted to sit at table and what delicacies they wanted us to serve them.

"Where've you guys been?" Noel demanded.

"Sorry!" I said.

Before I could answer Noel's question, Jorgia grabbed me by my shoulders and, pointing to the screen, shouted, "It's up!"

I looked at the white screen to see the opening images of our short film, with Sam rolling down the window of the car to look up at the facade of Elvira. I glanced around at the crowd and noticed that, even though most of them were on their phones or chatting with each other, more than a handful were actually watching our movie. I felt myself tearing up and wanted to just stay in that moment. But Noel snapped me out of it.

"Yo. You better get backstage!"

Jorgia and I ran to the back where Sir Li was already waiting.

"Hello, Cayt. Jorgia," Sir Li said, smiling nervously. "What did we get ourselves into?"

We waited with Sir Li backstage, resisting the urge to peek from behind the screen to see how the audience was reacting to our film. After a few more minutes, I heard the familiar score that Jorgia had made for the ending, followed by a respectable amount of applause. The sound made my heart swell.

Before long, Noel was introducing us over the microphone. Jorgia, Sir Li, and I made our way from behind the screen and up the stage to face the crowd, which was larger than I had anticipated. To our right, I heard a loud whoop and saw Law, Alex, and Hallie there at the very front, clapping and cheering for us. Jorgia waved at them but I could only manage a weak smile as we sat at the table, nerves finally kicking in. I wrinkled my nose and tried hard not to breathe in the various weird smells coming from the table. Beside me, Jorgia rubbed her palms together as if she was looking forward to our meal ahead.

We listened as Noel gave a recap about our fundraiser and the rules of the game before passing the microphone on to Sir Li. Then the three of us took turns to enumerate the items on the table—to collective "yucks" and gags.

"How much did you say was raised for me to eat all of this?" Sir Li asked.

From beside the platform, Noel shouted, "Five thousand seven hundred!"

"Do your parents know this is how you're spending your allowance?" Sir Li asked the crowd. Then, sighing dramatically, he added, "The things we do for our students."

We all laughed.

"Teachers first!" Jorgia said cheerily as she turned the wheeled table top so that the bowl of Soup No. Five was right under Sir Li's nose. "Let's start you off with an appetizer of cold testicle soup."

Jorgia pulled out a card from the deck with Sir Li's name on it and, giggling, read the question aloud. "Sir Li: According to your Facebook profile, you are single. Among the high school faculty, so are Ms. Katigbak, Ms. Pangilinan, and Ms. Suarez. Which one of them are you most likely to ask out and why?"

The crowd roared as Sir Li turned a light shade of pink. "I can't answer that."

Taking a deep breath, he removed his mask and dipped his spoon into the bowl. In the background, the crowd was chanting, "Eat. Eat. Eat." The spoon was almost in Sir Li's mouth when, all of a sudden, he gagged and dropped the spoon back in the bowl.

"I can't!" Sir Li gasped.

The crowd laughed. Some chanted, "Spill. Spill. Spill."

"I'm not a picky eater," Sir Li began to explain. "But this is just… the oil has coagulated!"

I laughed. "I don't even know what that means!"

But beside me, Jorgia had joined in the crowd's chanting. "Spill. Spill. Spill."

"Alright, alright," Sir Li said, raising his hands in defeat.

The crowd was now cheering, and so were we. "Who is it?!?" I screamed at my teacher.

"Okay. So, they're all incredible, don't get me wrong. But… I can't believe I'm going to answer this… ("SAY IT!!!" we all shrieked). I'd ask Rita."

The crowd cheered and whistled and, now, Sir Li was absolutely red.

"Why?" I suddenly remembered to ask.

"*Greatsenseofhumor*," Sir Li practically blurted out.

When the laughter had died down, we continued playing. True to her word, Jorgia didn't answer any of the questions thrown at her, which meant we both had to eat a slice of boiled tongue and swallow a spoonful of frozen *bagoong*. I answered who my favorite teacher was (Mrs. Aguirre, but reassured Sir Li he was a very close second), while Sir Li refused to eat uncooked Spam in *dinuguan* sauce, choosing to admit he hadn't been on a date in three years and seven months instead. Finally, it was my turn again.

Sir Li turned the table so that Jorgia and I were now face-to-face with a glass of yellowish goo, complete with reusable metal straws. I wrinkled my nose at the shake made from fermented rice. I was used to eating *buro* as a side with fried fish but imagined it would be difficult to drink because of the texture. I looked at Jorgia beside me, beads of sweat visible on her forehead. This was the only time I've seen Jorgia look nervous. In fact, she looked like she was about to throw up.

"Last question, Cayt," Sir Li said, a huge grin on his face. Who knew teachers could be so vindictive?

"You have to get this," Jorgia whispered urgently. "I can't drink that stuff."

Sir Li took a card from the stack of questions for film club members. "'Here's the question. 'Hanging out with our parents in public often leads to socially awkward experiences.' So this is what my and Rita's future kids will think of us."

The crowd roared. Then Sir Li continued.

"'Hanging out with our parents in public often leads to socially awkward experiences. What is your most embarrassing moment courtesy of either of your parents?'"

My heart was pounding. There was a loud ringing in my ears. Without even meaning to, I saw flashes of Mom spanking Sam uncontrollably in the restaurant. Mom and me, running from my old classroom because somebody had called her *bagtit*. Mom grabbing me by my collar and punishing me in front of Mai and our neighbors. Mom in the tub. Mom driving like a maniac. Mom shouting at me. Mom crying to me. Mom.

"Cayt," I finally heard Jorgia say.

I looked up to see both Sir Li and Jorgia staring back at me. Keeping the microphone away, Sir Li whispered, "Are you okay?"

I nodded wordlessly. Instinctively, I looked around and immediately wished I hadn't. Some people in the crowd were whispering to each other, some were giving me funny looks. I returned my gaze to Jorgia, pleading for help. She nodded and patted my hand.

Taking the microphone from Sir Li, Jorgia said, "Since Sir Li didn't eat anything (some in the crowd booed while Sir Li repeatedly laughed and shouted "sorry"), I think Cayt and I are gonna take one for the team and drink that shake."

A familiar voice in the crowd whooped. I gave Law a grateful look.

"Drink. Drink. Drink," some people began to chant.

Jorgia and I clinked straws before dipping them into the glass and taking a sip of the buro. Half a second later, we were both hurling into our own brown bags. I could hear the crowd cheering while I retched.

Sir Li handed us some paper towels and, after Jorgia and I had cleaned ourselves up, even nibbled voluntarily on a habanero pepper which, judging from the way he cried and pounded on the table for milk or water, must have been radioactive. By the time he had finished, every person in the crowd was chanting, "Super Li! Super Li!"

As the next student film played out on the white screen, the three of us trooped backstage, relieved that our ordeal was over. When we got there, Mrs. Aguirre was already waiting for her turn at the table. Noel clapped Jorgia and me on the shoulders and bumped fists with Sir Li.

"Nailed that, Sir!"

Sir Li was pink again as he smiled. After congratulating us on our fundraiser, he hurriedly bid us goodbye "before I get asked to sub for someone."

Law came rushing over. "You did great, guys!"

"Thanks for being our number one cheer dancer," Jorgia teased.

"Ha-ha," Law said. "You guys wanna get lunch or are you still full from the buro you just threw up?"

I watched as Jorgia punched Law playfully on the arm.

We said goodbye to Noel and the others and made our way to the nearby bathrooms to wash up. On the way there, I noticed some of the Lorenzo kids whispering as we passed by. I looked at Jorgia and Law, both of whom seemed to be oblivious to it as they argued which kiosk to hit for lunch. Jorgia and I walked into the bathrooms while Law waited outside.

"How bad was I," I began as I washed my face, "back there?"

"Hmm?" Jorgia mumbled as she gargled. "Don't worry. You only spaced for a sec."

We continued in silence. But I kept seeing the faces of the Lorenzo kids in my head. As we stepped out of the bathroom and into the hallway where Law was waiting, I couldn't help but bring it up again.

"I could've sworn people were giving me funny looks."

"That's probably just how they look," Jorgia said, chuckling. "You're reading too much into it."

"Oh okay, so I'm just being paranoid?"

"That's not what I said. Cayt, come on. Don't be like that."

"Like what?" I challenged, feeling myself unravel. "What shouldn't I be like, Jorgia?"

"Nothing! Can we just chill, please?"

"Like mental? That's what you were gonna say, right?" I accused.

"No! Of course, not!"

"Guys, what's going on?" I heard the echo of Law's voice ask from miles away.

"I bet you were thinking it," I insisted.

All this time, I thought Jorgia understood. That she accepted me. But maybe she was only tolerating me. And just like the others, she would leave once it got too much.

"I wasn't! Cayt, why are you doing this? I don't wanna argue with you here."

"Guys, maybe we should—"

"—I'm sorry if you think I'm acting mental. Heck, maybe I am!" I spat. "Not as if I can help it, what with me being stuck with a mom who wants to kill herself, y'know?"

"You *really* wanna talk about this here?" Jorgia's voice had risen to match mine.

"Yeah, I really do," I said without thinking.

"Fine. You wanna know what's mental? What's mental is you don't have to be stuck. You have a choice in all this but, for some reason, you're not doing anything about it!"

"Oh 'coz it's just sooo easy! I wonder why we never thought of bringing my Mom to the hospital against her will?!"

"Well you could get help for yourself. But you don't. Maybe because you like having somebody to blame if you blow things up the way you're doing right now."

When Jorgia said that, I felt something inside me snap.

"Who are you to judge *me*? You have no idea what it's like, okay?! So stop acting like you know anything and just buzz off."

The moment I said it, my soul was torn in two. Half of me regretted it and immediately wanted to take it back. But the other half—the one that felt as strong and angry as a dozen hurricanes—simply would not let me. What I said may not have been kind, but it was certainly true. Nobody can possibly understand what it felt like to be me.

Not knowing what else I could do, I made a run for it. I shoved past Law and a few other people, not caring if I had knocked anyone to the ground. Forget them all, I thought, seething with anger towards Jorgia and the whole world.

And Mom.

And myself.

I ran until I made it to the parking lot and, when I couldn't run anymore, kicked a trash bin and sent it flying towards a grimy sedan. I bent over to catch my breath, holding onto my knees. And that was when I noticed that my hands were shaking uncontrollably.

I clenched my fists to keep them from trembling. Then I let out a loud, frustrated scream that a part of me hoped someone would hear—but deep down knew nobody would.

WRITING ON THE WALL

It's official: I've lost my mind.

There was no other way to explain how I could've possibly said the things I did to the one person who stood by me and accepted me when anybody else would've run away. I didn't even understand why I did it. All I knew was that it had happened and, worse, there was something of an ugly monster inside me that enjoyed doing it. A monster that found relief in hurting another person—if only so they could feel how much pain it was in too.

I was afraid to find out how much that temporary relief would cost me.

The moment I got home from the fair, I deactivated all my accounts. And throughout the school fair holiday, I stayed offline and hid my phone so I wouldn't have to read any chats or be tempted to stalk any of my schoolmates. But most of all, so that I wouldn't end up sending Jorgia any of the sorry-I'm-an-evil-loser messages I had been trying to write since I came to my senses last night. Because none of them would ever be good enough.

I could never be good enough.

Naturally, I couldn't tell anyone at home what had happened. Mom didn't need another reason to mope or get angry, and Dad's plate was way too full. While we lay in bed, I considered Sam for a second. She had already fallen asleep, her tiny paws clutching at a star-shaped pillow in a death grip. She looked so at peace. I bet all she worried about was what she'd buy for recess every day, or what game to play with her friends while waiting for the school bus to pick her up.

I noticed that Sam's hands had rainbow-colored pen streaks all over them. How many times in the past month had I seen the same marks on her palms and stubby fingers? I went to the bathroom and dampened a towel, then gently rubbed my sister's hands clean.

Too young, I thought, positioning Sam's hand back on her pillow once I had finished. My sister couldn't even remember to wash up after herself. She couldn't possibly understand what I was going through. It was silly of me to even think I could talk to her about the impending doom that was Tuesday morning.

When I got to school, I went straight to the library. *Pet Sematary* was still there, looking like it hadn't been touched since I picked it up months ago. I flipped mindlessly through its yellowed pages until the first warning bell, when I had no choice but to drag myself to the classroom.

I kept my eyes trained on my feet so that I wouldn't see either Jorgia or the looks behind the murmuring that had broken out the moment I stepped inside the room. I scuttled to my row and sank low in my seat, avoiding Law's eyes or attempts at small talk. I held my breath for recess, when I could be alone again. When the bell rang for break, I darted out of my seat like a firecracker and ate my snack right outside the deserted library, timing myself so that I could sneak back into class just as everyone else had settled into their seats.

I repeated the same strategy for lunch later that day, using the time I would've normally spent chatting with Jorgia to study for next week's exams instead. And after class, while waiting for the bus at the front gate, I buried my face in my math book and wore earphones that weren't plugged into anything, just so I could focus on my exercises.

When I got to a particularly difficult equation, I wrinkled my nose and, desperate for a break, found myself looking up. Just then, Jorgia was passing by, with Alex and Hallie at each side. Our eyes met for the briefest second. I looked back down at my books as if I had been stung and did not dare take my eyes away from my equations again until the school bus had arrived.

With no Jorgia and Law to go to Profanitea with, and film club on a brief hiatus to let members rest, I had no other option but to bury myself in schoolwork. At the rate I was going, I could probably take next year's tests too. I guess that was the silver lining to being a loner again. Before I knew it, Friday night had come and I had finished all of Sir Li's practice sheets. Too bad I didn't have Law to check my answers though.

I crawled towards my bag on the floor, looking for my highlighter.

That's weird, I thought to myself after I had turned my bag inside out and yielded zero highlighters. I seemed to be going through them faster than usual but I could've sworn I still had a green one yesterday. I rolled off the bed and peered under to see if it was there. Nada. Oh well. Maybe that's the sign to call it a night.

I climbed back into bed and was about to switch off the night light when I noticed Sam's hands. They were covered in what was unmistakably the same shade of mint as my highlighter. Curious, I tiptoed out of bed and checked her bag. There I saw around three dozen markers including all of the highlighters that I thought I had lost. I flipped through her notebooks, expecting to see them covered in rainbow marks but they were all a pristine white and looked like they had hardly been opened. Which was also suspicious.

After taking back my pastel highlighter, I put Sam's bag in order and got back to bed, re-reading my notes until I fell asleep.

By the time I woke up and went down to the kitchen, Dad, Mom, and Sam were already clearing their plates.

"Late night?" Dad asked as he set a plate of rice and toasted adobo flakes in front of me.

I nodded, hastily saying grace before I dug into my breakfast.

"Exams next week, right?"

I nodded again.

"Figures. I don't think you've been this focused on school since…" Dad trailed off, suddenly interested in watching Sam and Mom walk out of the kitchen.

The last time I was this studious was also the last time I lost all my friends.

"I know you'll do well, Cayt," Dad picked up. "You're a good girl, you always have been."

"Whoa. That came out of nowhere," I said, putting the back of my hand on Dad's forehead and pretending to check if he had a fever.

"Don't act like this is the first time I've told you that," Dad chuckled as he swatted at my hand. "Now finish up. Lunch is in an hour."

"What's for lunch?" I was almost afraid to ask.

"Pizza," Dad said, grinning.

"Whoaaaa. Big time!" I teased.

"Yeah, yeah," he said. With one last eye roll, Dad left me to my own devices in the kitchen so he could watch over Mom doing the laundry.

I gobbled up the rest of my breakfast as fast as I could, hating the feeling of eating on my own even when I was at home. As a result, my insides soon after felt like they were being twisted around by an invisible hand. I walked up the spiral stairs slowly, hunched over and clutching at my stomach in discomfort.

When I got to our room, I heard Sam humming the chorus of *Permission to Dance*. I couldn't immediately locate where she was though. I followed the sound of her off-key singing until they led me to the wardrobe, its doors slightly ajar.

I gulped and hesitated for a second, remembering that vintage horror movie I had seen with Ate Fe about a monster child hiding in a closet. After reminding myself that it was just a movie, I swung the door open and shouted, "Boo!"

"AAAARGH!" Sam shrieked.

Once I had stopped laughing and Sam had run out of frilly socks to throw at me, I stepped back to inspect the crime scene before me. There, at the bottom of the closet, sat my younger sister, surrounded by a dozen or so markers. Behind Sam, I caught a glimpse of her abstract handiwork through the curtain of her school dresses. I moved to sweep the clothes aside but Sam resisted, pulling her dresses back so that they were in mortal danger of being ripped in half.

"What did you do, Sam?!"

"It's nothing!"

"This isn't nothing. Writing on walls is vandalism, you know."

"Not if it's *your* wall," she insisted.

The girl had a point. We had grown up writing on our own walls, after all—but only in the Facebook sense and not quite so literal as this.

"Come on, won't you show *ate*?" I asked sweetly, changing my tactics.

Sam considered me for a second, raising her left eyebrow. I didn't even know she could do that already. She had grown up in this small way without me noticing.

"Fine, but don't judge. Remember: I don't have formal training," she said, pushing back her dresses to reveal her wooden canvas.

"It's like you judged yourself, you know?" I teased as I moved forward for a closer look.

I couldn't understand what I was looking at at first, blinded as I was by all the colors. Man, if I didn't know Sam had made this, I would've said somebody high on drugs had. After studying it a bit more, I was able to make out a teepee and three troll-looking people with long hair (which I assumed meant they were girls) inside, reading a huge book as they lay on their stomachs.

That was us. Me and Sam and Mom.

I crouched next to Sam inside the open wardrobe to scrutinize her painting further. I was so close that I could smell the dizzying alcohol scent of the markers. I noticed another troll peeking from behind the teepee. He was wearing the same white shirt, jeans, and leather sandals that was Dad's daily uniform. The image of our family made me smile. Even though we didn't really look human here.

"Wow, this is really good, Sam," I said, ruffling my sister's hair, as we crawled out of the closet. "I hope you're putting in as much effort on your homework though."

Sam stuck her tongue out at me. I kicked at her playfully and shooed her away.

I started picking up the markers and putting back the caps on them. And that was when I noticed it. Even though her painting was colorful, it was predominantly dark except inside the teepee. Around the family was a cosmic mess of deep blues and purples and reds. It was an image that worried me somehow.

Sam came back just then to take a snap of her masterpiece with the tablet. I watched as she cropped the photo and uploaded it onto her profile.

"Why hide it from us if you're gonna show the rest of your friends, anyway?"

Sam shrugged as a way of answering, before heading downstairs and disappearing from my sight.

I gathered the pens and shut the closet doors, taking my own highlighters from the bunch before tossing the rest into Sam's bag.

I wonder what kind of comments the kids were leaving on Sam's photo? They better be good, I thought. I took out my phone and, with some hesitation, reactivated my socials. Ignoring all my messaging apps for fear of what had been sent to me—or that there weren't any at all—I went straight to Sam's profile.

There were already quite a number of likes and hearts. And it had only been a few minutes too. Way to go, Sam! She may have a use yet, I thought, smirking.

I scrolled down and saw that Sam had posted a couple other doodles, but none quite as good as the one she had drawn on the inside of our closet. I scrolled some more, past a bunch of her schoolmates' vlogs, until I came across a short status from that Monday when our parents had had a fight.

Why is life hard?

If I hadn't known better, I might've rolled my eyes. What else could students from Lorenzo—especially students Sam's age—stress about, apart from their grades?

But then Sam *had* gone through a lot the past months. Out of nowhere, I remembered how Sam had struggled to break free from Mom's grip as she spanked her in that restaurant. How she had quivered and kept silent in Mom's presence in the weeks that followed. How she had clung to me when Mom first came up with the idea to go to the mall. And how she had asked Dad if Mom didn't love her anymore.

I was suddenly overcome with both pity and admiration for my little sister.

I looked at Sam's post again and noticed that there were a lot of sad face reactions, along with a number of "LUV U," "HANG IN THERRRR," "smile!!!," and "ikr" comments. But there was one from a kid whose name I didn't recognize that said: *"bagtit ti manang."*

I tossed my phone on Sam's bed as if it had burned my hand. *Bagtit.*

I had never even dared to utter the word aloud the moment we left our old house. I had ripped that page out of my mental dictionary. I had threatened to have Sam taken away by fearsome policemen if she attempted to parrot our neighbors one more time.

Crazy. I wanted nothing to do with it.

But crazy had been with us when we moved. And now, I thought as I inched cautiously towards my phone and looked at Sam's post again, it seemed as if crazy had taken over our entire home.

ERASERS

I had major tests coming up so, naturally, I felt like I could throw up any moment.

Other times, I found myself imagining what it would be like to get some sort of injury and be exempted from exams as a result. But I guess I wasn't too desperate because the weekend passed without me placing my hands on top of the burner or provoking our landlady's dog to bite me.

I couldn't really bring myself to, especially after reading Sam's post.

It might've been too little and too late, but I put off some last-minute reviewing on Sunday for my sister's sake. I realized that I had been ignoring Sam all these months and that I should've been more present for her. To make up for lost time, I built her a blanket fort which I think looked way better (in an eclectic, mishmash way) than that store-bought teepee we had briefly owned. I let Sam choose all the shows she wanted to watch while we cuddled together inside our fort and, when she wasn't looking, hid packs of gummy bears in her school bag and her side of the closet.

Sam seemed so happy, like gummy bears could erase her worries just like that. But instead of it making me feel just as giddy, the thought saddened me all the more.

If it only took a little to make my sister happy, then things must've been really bad for her to feel that life was hard. Sam was only eight. The only thing that should be difficult for her now was homework and tying her own shoelaces (which I only learned to do when I was nine).

So, before I called it a night, I mustered up all of my courage (by screaming at myself that I was the *ate*, for crying out loud), and sought Dad out in his makeshift office at the dining table, showing him a photo of Sam's wall and her recent posts. With a heavy sigh, Dad dutifully closed his ledgers and ascended up the stairs to our room—me right behind him—to ask Sam about what she had written.

"Hey kiddo," Dad said as he sat on the edge of Sam's pullout bed, where my sister had already tucked herself in. "Your *ate* told me about your mural in the closet."

Sam looked at me, her eyes turning into slits.

"Don't worry!" Dad said, laughing. "She didn't do that to get you in trouble. She actually told me because she thought it was really good. Mind showing me your work, buddy?"

I watched Sam consider this for a bit before throwing aside the covers and leaping from the bed. She sprinted to our closet and held the door open, gesturing toward the interior like a magician's assistant. Dad followed her and I heard the sound of plastic hangers clacking against each other as he pushed our dresses aside to get a good look at Sam's painting. After that, Dad proceeded to shower her with maybe one too many compliments. Sam looked pretty smug by the time Dad finished, the big grin plastered on her face showing all her milk teeth.

"So what was the inspiration behind this?" Dad asked, as if he were interviewing a professional artist.

"I dunno… that was just what I felt like drawing at the time, I guess," Sam said, shrugging as she crawled back into bed. "I like saying how I feel with colors and pictures."

Wow, I thought, looking at Sam with a newfound curiosity. That was kind of how I felt with my films too.

"Was that also how you felt when you posted on Facebook about life being hard?"

"Uhm… Sort of, yeah," Sam answered, avoiding Dad's gaze and shooting a look towards the open bedroom door before looking down at her tiny hands and fidgeting with her blanket. Dad sat beside Sam again and placed a hand over hers.

"I'm sorry we didn't notice sooner, Sam," Dad said, his voice smooth and low. "But if you ever have a hard time with anything again–anything at all–you can come to me or your *ate*, okay? We're just here for you."

Sam nodded, giving Dad and me a weak smile before hugging Dad around his waist.

"Hey, give me some of that!" I said, jumping onto the bed and forcing my way into the group hug.

"Aack! Geroff, *ate*!" came Sam's muffled voice.

All in all, I was convinced that it was a day well spent, even if it meant it was also a day not spent reviewing. Come Wednesday morning, though, when we were being handed out our test papers, I was a lot less certain.

On exam days, we were always dismissed at noon. This was also the case in my old school. I guess it was universal practice to cram for the next tests at the last opportunity available. And that was exactly what I did. Science, Social Science, English, Religion, Reading, Filipino. And, finally, Math.

I was still re-reading my notes during recess on Friday when Law sat beside me on the library steps, books in tow.

I gaped at him, dumbfounded. How many times had Jorg and I tried to drag him out of the classroom and into the cafeteria with us, only for him to refuse every single time?

Without a word, Law flipped open his books and started reading beside me. But after a minute or two, I figured he wasn't reading at all because 1) he wasn't flipping the pages, and 2) he was staring out at the open field across us, where a few other kids were reviewing too.

"Nervous about the exam?" Law asked, breaking the silence. Also unusual.

"I was trying not to be until you reminded me," I admitted.

Law chuckled and, for about half a minute, we both pretended to be reviewing again. Then he spoke once more, his voice as deep and calming as ever.

"I know I'm not cool, and I don't get any of your movie references the way Jorgia does. And obviously I'm not a girl. But . . ." Law began to say, "I'm here still. You don't have to avoid everyone and you don't have to be alone… Unless you want to, of course."

If a look could convey gratitude, I hoped mine did now as I looked at Law.

I never really gave him that much thought, to be honest. But he's been a real friend. Helping us out with our film. Not hating on me or Jorg even though we'd sometimes exclude him, especially about Mom stuff. Bringing extra sheets of paper because he knew I always ran out. It was kind of an honor that he left the comfort of the classroom to tell me this now.

"Wow. Thanks, Law," was all I could say.

Law grinned. Then, taking a deep breath, he said, "I saw your sister's post from that day. You wanna, uhm… talk?"

I almost laughed, certain that I had seen his eyes twitch during that last bit. "No, I'm good."

"Oh. Okay then, if you're sure. So should we go—?'

"—It's just that I'm so embarrassed by what I did at the fair. What I said to Jorgia…"

"I think you shouted at her to, uhm, mind her own business?"

"That's a very Disney Channel way of putting it," I said, chuckling. "I was so… self-obsessed? Is that the word? I was so busy thinking about what other people thought of me. I forgot to be a good sister. And a good friend."

"Well, aren't we all self-obsessed from time to time? But something I've learned being around you guys… we should only think about what the people who love us think," Law said.

"Deep," I said.

"Just rambling," Law said, smiling. "Well, that's what I thought when I auditioned for dance. Told myself 'Law, Cayt and Jorg said you had the moves. That's what matters.'"

We laughed.

"You really do."

"Thank you, thank you," Law said, bowing comically.

We smiled silently at each other. Then Law spoke again. "You should talk to her."

I shook my head and looked away. "I was such a jerk."

"I don't know if *jerk* is the word I'd use. I mean, maybe the way you cursed at Jorgia was out of line. And you did bowl over innocent bystanders who just happened to be at the wrong place, at the wrong time… But nothing we don't see online every day," Law teased.

I punched him in the arm.

"You needed to say some things. I don't know the whole story but whatever it is you're going through… Well if you ask me, it was good that you cried for help," Law continued, but seriously now, in a way that almost unnerved me. "Talk to Jorg. You guys are crazy about each other."

I didn't flinch at the word this time.

"Not in a lesbian way or anything. I think. I mean, if you are, that's okay too."

I laughed at Law. "You can stop talking now."

"Okay, sorry. I'm not good at this stuff," Law said sheepishly.

"Actually, I think you are," I said, smiling.

Just then, the warning bell rang. Law and I gathered our things and started walking briskly towards our class room, a lightness in our steps.

"Good luck to us," Law whispered as we took our seats. Mrs. Aguirre walked to the front of the room and, with a heavy thud, dropped onto the table an ominous stack of brown sheets that were our Math tests.

I smiled and whispered "good luck" back, my heart feeling a little less heavy.

Then I saw all the numbers on my paper and couldn't help but wonder why Law hadn't gone to see me in the library yesterday so we could've still reviewed for Math together. I had lost so much time scrolling for relevant tutorials on @onlinekyne's TikTok.

Can't win them all, I told myself as I uncapped my pen.

I wasn't even halfway through the test when I noticed that I had nearly drenched my exam sheets just by holding them between my sweaty palms. And I had a feeling it was no longer the quest to figure out the value of X that was making me so anxious.

"Talk to her." I kept hearing Law's voice in my mind.

Another voice in my mind (still a sane one, I hoped) answered, "Will you freakin' let me finish this test?!"

That made Law's voice retreat, tail between its legs. I went back to item number eighty-seven.

Oh shoot, oh shoot. What the heck is Y now??

Dear Lord, help me, I thought desperately. I promise to be good and sleep on time and to never curse again or join in the laughter when somebody makes fun of any of my teachers, but especially Mrs. Castro, behind their backs.

After five minutes had passed on the wall clock above the blackboard, I still hadn't made any progress on the equation.

Oh, fine! I'll talk to her. Just let me figure it out, I pleaded.

I trained my eyes on the problem and realized I had misread it all along. I re-did my solution and ticked off what I hoped was the right choice, before moving on to number eighty-eight. I kept scribbling and counting numbers on my fingers until I finished my paper, just a few minutes short of the bell.

My fate was now out of my hands. I put down my pen and, with a sigh of relief, passed my paper to the person in front of me.

All around me, my classmates were rejoicing at the end of our exams, screaming and cheering and laughing nervously. Mrs. Aguirre waved us off, admonishing us to enjoy our weekend. "Time to celebrate, class! Have fun while you can because, next week, you're gonna reap what you sowed."

Half the class groaned.

"Why'd you have to remind us, Miss?" Hallie asked.

"Only feel bad if you didn't actually study," Mrs. Aguirre answered, laughing as half of the class groaned yet again.

"Alright! Come on, bring out those erasers I gave you."

Mrs. Aguirre sat casually on the desk and waited as we rummaged through our bags. I got mine from my pen bag. It had hardly been touched.

"Why'd you think I gave you those things when most of you use correction tape? Or just scrawl over the words to confuse me sometimes?"

I laughed. Guilty as charged.

"We still have two quarters left. Now, I'm not saying you should always keep waiting until the last minute to make up for your grades but…" she paused for emphasis. "BUT. You can always start over. There are very few things in this world that can't be fixed or made better when you set your minds to it."

I stared at Mrs. Aguirre as she addressed our class. Just before she turned around to write on the blackboard, I swear I saw her wink in my direction.

I had a feeling she wasn't just talking about my Math exam.

Once we had been dismissed, I got up, grit my teeth, and clenched my fists, ready to approach Jorgia as she packed up her bag.

"H-hi," I stuttered.

Jorgia looked up and hesitated for a second before saying "hi" back.

It wasn't very enthusiastic but at least she didn't ignore me completely, right? I took a deep breath and wasn't quite sure what I was about to say next but, whatever it could've been, I didn't get a chance to say it.

Alex bumped past me and, grabbing Jorgia's bag from her desk, murmured something to her. I didn't hear the exact words but was able to make out something like "this is crazy."

Jorgia didn't budge from her place. But Alex's words set me off and, before I knew it, I was sprinting out the room, jostling past dozens of Lorenzo students just like I did at the fair.

I didn't wait for the school bus. I couldn't keep still or stay in one place so I walked home instead. When I got there, all sweaty and tired, Mom and Dad were at the kitchen, getting lunch ready.

"Hi, hun," Dad greeted me all cheery, looking up as he continued to set the table. "How come Sam got here before you?"

"Oh, I decided to walk," I answered as I sat down.

"Wash your hands and call your sister. Food's almost ready," Mom said.

I got up and dragged my feet to the bottom of the stairs where I shouted "SAM!" before returning to the kitchen and slumping back down on my chair.

"Math was that hard, huh?" Dad asked, sitting down on the table across me.

"Math… and other things," I said.

"It'll be okay, Cayt. I'm sure you did well," Dad said, giving me a small smile.

"I think I'll pass, at the very least."

"At least?" Mom asked, her forehead wrinkling. "I expect more than a passing grade."

"I doubt it'll be just a passing grade," Dad said, winking at me. "You have been an overachiever since you were a baby. Pooped more than any other infant I saw!"

"Ha-ha." I laughed sarcastically and narrowed my eyes at Dad.

"That better be the case," Mom said underneath her breath, but still loud enough for me to hear.

And it really ticked me off.

"What is wrong with you? Can't you be supportive for once?" I asked, my voice rising.

"Cayt—" Dad warned.

"Me?" Mom asked. "I didn't do anything."

"That's right, you didn't," I answered, talking over Dad, who had held up his hands and was motioning for us to calm down. But I couldn't.

"Where *were* you when I needed help with my studies? Or when Sam did?"

"I was right here."

"No, you weren't. You were inside your freakin' head! You have no right to be disappointed in me because you didn't help me at all—not one bit."

"CAYT, ENOUGH!" Dad roared. "Go to your room."

I turned around and began to stomp out of the kitchen.

"No, get back here!" Mom demanded.

I stopped walking and turned around to look at her. Mom's face was livid. A vein throbbed in her neck.

"Anna, no. You need to sit. Cayt, go!"

"No, stay! You need to hear this," Mom spat. She pointed a shaking finger at me so that there was no question in my mind that it was me she was referring to.

"You're ungrateful. And you're weak. You want to work in film like I did? Well, guess what, you don't have what it takes!"

My heart stopped beating right there and then. So how could I have still heard the rest of what she had to say?

"I regret ever having you."

I shook my head, unwilling to believe it, as I stared at Mom's face. It seemed calm, no longer unbridled by emotion—as if she had simply stated fact.

As if her words didn't crush her the way they did me. Why did she hate me so much? Well, I wasn't gonna let her be the only one.

"I hate you," I said.

I was surprised that the words had come to my lips as quickly as they had formed in my thoughts. Then I was seized by a primal desire to draw blood. To hurt her as much as she had hurt me. So I said it again, but louder this time.

"I hate you!"

"CAYT—"

Dad had his hands on my shoulders now and was pushing me out of the kitchen.

But I wouldn't let him stop me. Even as he tried to block her from my view, I squirmed out of Dad's grip so I could look into her eyes as I said it:

"Go ahead and kill yourself. I don't want you in my life either."

Eyes stinging, I turned around and fled past a petrified Sam. I threw our front door wide open and ran out into the streets without a care for which direction I went, as long as it was far, far away from the woman who had ceased to be my mother.

PATCH

I must've looked wild when I showed up at Cinema Paradiso. My uniform was disheveled and my face was grimy from having walked the entire way because I didn't have my phone or wallet or anything at all with me. I just knew I had to go to the one place I could think of that still held a sliver of hope for me.

"I did something. Something… bad."

"What?" Jorgia asked, looking wary from behind the old-fashioned ticket booth.

I gulped for air. I couldn't speak. Saying it aloud would make it real. I caught my reflection on the window of the booth. Tears had left clear streaks down the dirt on my cheeks.

"Stay there."

I watched wordlessly as Jorgia got up and approached a young guy wearing the same shirt as her's. He nodded and took the seat from behind the booth. Then Jorgia pulled me to the deserted snack bar. She sat cross-legged on the floor behind the counter and pulled me down so I'd do the same.

"What's going on, Cayt?"

Jorgia's eyes were trained on me, the crease between her brows telling me she was worried. For me. Why was she even speaking to me? Even if I had been banking on it, I didn't actually deserve her kindness towards me. I was a bad person. Just the thought made me cry all over again.

"I'm sorry!" I sputtered uncontrollably. "I'm so sorry."

"Shhh!" she said, looking around us. Then, more gently, she added, "It's okay. I get it."

I shook my head, sobbing. It wasn't okay.

"It's okay. I swear, Cayt… We're alright."

I looked up at Jorgia. Though her brows were still furrowed, her eyes were smiling. It felt like she meant it. I tried to muster a smile back but my lips wouldn't cooperate.

"What happened?" she asked.

"I, uh . . ." I stammered, trying to figure out where to start. "I ran away."

Was it running away if you didn't pack your clothes?

"Oh. Okay. Well… I guess that's not too bad, right?"

Then, probably in an attempt to lighten the mood, Jorgia added, "For a second there I thought you had killed someone and had come to ask for my help with the body."

I burst out into tears.

"Oh! Shoot! Uhm… okay. Uhm… you didn't, right? Cayt? But, uhm… no judgment?"

I didn't answer.

I had told her—the woman who had once attempted suicide, who had practically admitted to me that she was considering it again—to kill herself.

Well, she deserved it, I thought bitterly. She deserved it for hating me first. If she didn't care to have me in her life, then I didn't want her in my life either.

So why was I crying? Why did my chest ache so much that it burned with hatred, not for her, but for myself and for what I had done?

Jorgia looked at me, waiting with bated breath.

"I… I might as well have," I managed to say between sobs.

And Jorgia held me there, behind dusty stacks of potato chips and candy, for I dunno how long until I had stopped crying. Then she whispered into my ear.

"I'm sorry. For everything you're going through, Cayt."

And that was all I needed to hear.

My sobs turned to sniffs and, finally, I felt like I could pull myself together. Jorgia grabbed a bottle of water from the shelf and handed it to me as I scooped myself up from the floor. I downed the bottle in two gulps.

"You okay now?" Jorgia asked.

I didn't answer.

"Stupid question, of course you're not," Jorgia said, slapping her forehead and rolling her eyes at herself. "Not yet, anyway."

I gave her a weak smile. It was all that I could muster.

"I wish things could be better, Cayt."

I nodded, biting my lip. I wished it too.

Jorgia grabbed a bag of corn chips from the shelf and tore it open, offering it to me before lifting herself up from the floor and telling me to wait while she asked for permission to leave.

From where I sat, munching on stale chips, I could still see the framed movie posters that lined the hallway of Paradiso. How many times had I imagined my own movie poster hanging side by side with *Tapang* or *Mana*? But it seemed so unimportant now. It was a distant dream that didn't matter quite as much as Sam being able to paint happy drawings, or Dad being free to use the big knives when he's cooking, or me not being afraid to talk about Mom, or Mom being happy and wanting to still live even when she isn't.

But how can any of these dreams come true?

And where do I even begin?

The moment I asked myself, I knew.

Maybe I had just been afraid of how it would make me look and what other people would say. Or that it wouldn't help at all. But I had known all along.

Half an hour later, I was back at Lorenzo. After a quick stop by Jorgia's house so I could wash my face and change out of my uniform, the two of us made our way to the school's second-floor lounge, where Mrs. Aguirre was waiting for us right outside.

She looked kindly at us, a crinkle in her eyes.

"Thanks for seeing us, Miss," Jorgia said.

"Thank you for calling me," Mrs. Aguirre said back. Then she tilted her head towards me and asked, "Would you like to sit with me inside, Cayt?"

I nodded. I took a step forward. Then another, until Mrs. Aguirre and I were walking side by side, making our way inside the lounge.

I had never been here before. It looked cozy, if not a bit outdated, with its butter-yellow walls and cushy floral sofas. There was a shelf with a curious mix of books and board games and art materials and toys.

"Sit anywhere you like, Cayt. I have some iced tea here for you," Mrs. Aguirre said as she poured me out a glass from the pitcher on the coffee table.

I took it and made to sit on the couch but stopped midway. "Should I lie down? In the movies, the patient lies down."

"Oh, you're not a patient, Cayt. And I'm not a doctor. But feel free to lie down if you like."

Mrs. Aguirre pulled up an arm chair. I tried to lie down on the sofa but it felt really weird so I sat up and hugged one of the pillows instead.

"Would you like some more iced tea?" Mrs. Aguirre asked, refilling my empty glass. I hadn't even noticed that I had finished it all.

"Oh. Okay," I said sheepishly, taking the glass and downing half of it in a gulp. "Thanks."

"You seem very thirsty."

"Yeah, I uh… I guess I'm just tired."

"From what I heard, you seem to have done a bit of walking."

"I guess," I said, looking away from Mrs. Aguirre.

"Mm-hmm," I heard her say.

Then neither she nor I said anything, which made me feel a bit uneasy. Like it was still my turn to speak.

"Well, I did run a bit," I found myself saying. Then, almost involuntarily, I laid back down on the sofa, propping my head up with the pillow before I continued to speak. "Maybe seven, eight K?"

"That's quite a distance."

"Yeah. I uh… went to the first place I could think of."

"You went to see Jorgia."

"Uh huh. Even though we weren't speaking."

"I had noticed that."

"You did, huh? Kinda hard to miss."

Mrs. Aguirre didn't respond. I shifted my head to see if maybe she had dozed off or was checking something on her phone, but she was just looking at me. Weird. I went back to staring at the ceiling.

"It's because of my mother," I finally said.

"What is?"

"My fight with Jorg… And life sucking."

I waited for Mrs. Aguirre to tell me that life didn't suck. But she didn't. She just sat there, listening, I assumed.

"She hates me, you know? My Mom… I guess, sometimes, I hate her, too."

Talking to the ceiling was easy. Ceilings couldn't judge you or tell you they thought you were horrible. And if they did, they'd probably have to collapse on you to get the point across, which was a win-win situation, in my opinion.

"What makes you feel that way?" the ceiling asked.

I paused.

She said that she regretted having me. How can I not hate her for that? But a part of me knew that, if she took it back, I would too. I blinked back the tears that had began to well in my eyes once more.

"I guess… I don't really hate her? Just what she did… and that she hurt me. Does that make sense?"

"It does. Sometimes," the ceiling started to say, "when a person we love hurts us and we don't understand why, it seems natural to want to hurt them back."

I held tightly onto the pillow, clutching it to my chest as if it were a lid that could keep the pain from overflowing.

"Sometimes we love someone so much that our hearts bleed when they hurt us."

A howl escaped from between my lips as I turned around on my stomach and pressed my face down on the cushions. How could I make my own mother love me again? I asked myself. And why *should* I have to?

Once I had run out of tears, I sat myself up on the couch and busied myself with arranging the cushions, too embarrassed to look Mrs. Aguirre in the eyes.

I trained my sight on the table instead, where she started pouring me another glass of iced tea. I took it and murmured "thank you" before drinking it all. I had finished the whole pitcher, apparently.

Mrs. Aguirre took my hands and held them in hers. They were very warm and soothing. Like my mother's once were.

I gulped.

"How can I make her not hate me anymore?"

Mrs. Aguirre's hands gave mine a squeeze.

"Cayt," she said to me, pausing, so that I had to look into her eyes. "Some people go through things that make them… lose control of themselves. It could be a loss, a big change, experiences in the past. Even a chemical imbalance or hormones. There are so many factors. And that could be why your Mom… said or did some things that hurt you."

I nodded. I had read that already somewhere. I knew that.

But why was it still difficult to believe?

"It's not because of you, Cayt… It's not your fault."

And the dam broke all over again.

At the end of my long conversation with Mrs. Aguirre, we agreed that she could call my parents and talk to them while I hung out at Jorgia's for a bit more. The sun had nearly set when Jorgia and I arrived at her house.

Just a few blocks off of Paradiso, their house was a small, weirdly shaped bungalow with an elliptical hallway that branched out into three bedrooms, a bathroom, the kitchen, and a messy dining and living room teeming with books and trophies and keepsakes and framed photos.

We plopped down on the sofa and perched our legs atop a wooden chest moonlighting as a coffee table and didn't speak for half an hour or so. It was only then when it dawned on me how dead tired I was.

I heard my stomach growl and realized I hadn't had anything since recess aside from stale chips, water, and iced tea.

Jorgia sniggered beside me when it growled again. "Hungry much?"

"I know I already owe you but… d'you have anything to eat?"

"Yeah, just go in the kitchen and get whatever," Jorgia said as she lay still on the sofa.

I guess being the friend of a person whose mom had issues could be just as tiring. I crawled to the other room, my hunger only beating my exhaustion by an inch. When I got there, though, I was surprised to see Jorgia's older sister, her electric blue hair tied behind her head in a very short ponytail. Jacqui was cooking something on the stove while consulting a YouTube video.

"Oh. Hi!" she said, pausing the video.

"Sorry!" I said and made to back out of the kitchen.

"No, it's fine. Stay! What d'you need? Is Jorgia there?" Jacqui peered out of the glass window of the kitchen door.

"Yeah. I was just gonna get some snacks… for us."

"Okay, help yourself," Jacqui said, gesturing towards the basket of fruits on the counter. Once she had turned her back to me, I grabbed the basket and the jar of peanut brittle beside it. Just as I was sneaking out of the kitchen, Jacqui unpaused her video and resumed following the instructions some lanky blonde guy in an apron was giving.

I set down the food at Jorgia's feet and immediately started devouring a banana.

"Your *ate*'s in there," I finally said after two bananas and a handful of brittle.

Jorgia rolled her eyes.

"Ugh. She's been cooking nonstop the past week. I think she's trying to prove to him how domestic she can be."

"So, is she?"

"No idea. She wouldn't let me taste any of it," Jorgia said bitterly as she gnawed on a large chunk of peanut brittle. "Probably sucks anyway."

Just then, Jacqui walked out of the kitchen, holding a glass tray between her hands and placing it gingerly on the dining table as if it were an urn that held the ashes of Jose Rizal or something. Just from the smell of the dish that had wafted towards us, I could tell that whatever she had made probably didn't suck at all.

"Don't touch this," she warned us before disappearing behind the kitchen door once more.

For the first time since we arrived, Jorgia got up from the sofa and walked towards the dining table. She frowned at the tray so much that I began to fear for its safety.

"Maybe you can ask her if you could have a bite," I suggested.

"No way. I am *not* asking her for anything," Jorgia said, turning her nose up from the tray and crashing back on the couch.

I watched as she began stuffing her face with more brittle. After a few minutes, Jacqui emerged from the other side of the hallway. She had already changed into a red dress, which I thought went really well with her blue hair that was now styled back down. She sat on an armchair and started putting on her boots.

"I'm going out to see Ian. It's our monthsary," she said.

"Shocker," Jorgia muttered underneath her breath.

"Mom said you can order food. There's money on top of the piano," Jacqui continued to say as she grabbed the glass tray from the dining table. Then, turning to me, she asked, "Cayt, right? Are you staying for dinner too?"

"Uhm… I'm not sure," I answered. I looked at Jorgia. "Did Mrs. Aguirre message yet?"

"Nope," Jorgia said, shaking her head.

"Mrs. Aguirre?" Jacqui repeated. She was by the front door now and held it open, pausing. "Isn't she the guidance counselor? Jorgia May, are you in trouble?"

"Adviser, dummy," Jorgia snapped back. "And no, we're not. Why don't you just leave already?"

"Jorg, if you did something—"

"I didn't, okay?! You're one to talk."

I watched as the two sisters glowered at each other and, for the briefest of seconds, imagined how this would be Sam and me in a few more years.

I cleared my throat. "Actually, *ate*… it's because of me."

Jacqui tore her eyes away from Jorgia and looked at me instead. "Don't cover for her!"

"No, it's not like that," I said, looking down at my feet. "I uh… I kinda ran away from home."

"Oh."

I heard the door close with a soft thud. Then, the clacking of boots and the scraping of a chair on the tiled floor before Jacqui's voice broke the silence.

"You wanna talk about it?"

"She already did," Jorgia butted in. "That's why we're waiting for Aguirre. So you can go ahead with your date already."

"Can you stop being an ass for a sec?"

"You're the one who accused me of getting in trouble!"

"Well, that's 'coz—" Jacqui started to say but then stopped mid-sentence.

Maybe she had noticed, just as I had, that Jorgia's eyes were glistening already. I watched Jacqui take a deep breath and set the glass tray back down on the table before squeezing herself next to Jorgia on the sofa even though there was so much room elsewhere.

"I'm sorry for thinking you were in trouble," Jacqui said as she hugged her sister tight.

"*Geroffme!*"

"Say 'it's okay!' Say it or I won't let go!"

"No. No!" Jorgia squealed, trying to wriggle out of her sister's reach. But I could tell she wasn't trying that hard. "All right. Fine!! Now get off!"

Jacqui released Jorgia from underneath her and pulled herself up from the sofa.

"Jorg, why don't you set the table while I cook some rice?"

"What about *Iiiiaaaan?*" Jorgia asked, taunting in a singsong voice.

"Eh," Jacqui said as she slipped off her boots. "There's always next month."

We had dinner soon as the rice was done, which was a good thing or else my gut would've eaten itself whole already. Jacqui's ox tongue in tomato sauce was really good. We had nearly finished the whole thing when Jorgia suddenly got up and ran to the kitchen, returning with a ceramic bowl. We looked at her, puzzled, as she spooned a heaping serving of lengua into it.

"What are you doing?" Jacqui finally asked.

"Saving some for Ian," Jorgia said, shrugging as if it was no big deal.

Jacqui and I smiled at each other. Then she got up to give Jorgia another bear hug.

"Do you like *Iiiaan* now?" Jacqui teased, copying how Jorgia said it a while ago.

"Don't push it," Jorg said, holding the glass bowl away from Jacqui, "or else I'm gonna take it back and finish this all."

Jacqui laughed, palms up in surrender. "You got it, baby sis."

While we were cleaning up, Jorgia received a call from Mrs. Aguirre saying I could sleep over and my parents would pick me up tomorrow. So we spent the rest of the evening looking at Jorg and Jacqui's baby pictures—they actually had printouts—and taking turns telling stories from our childhood. They loved when I told them about going fishing or riding carabaos in our old farm with my family.

Jacqui let us crash in her room for the night ("This never happens," Jorgia told me). I lay on a mattress on the floor, while the two sisters curled up next to each other on Jacqui's bed.

As I dozed off to sleep, their giggling and whispering growing ever fainter with each passing second, I had the vaguest feeling that, maybe, I had actually done something good today.

SQUAD

I wasn't sure how things would be from that point on. I was only certain that I wanted them to change.

Dad showed up at Jorgia's driveway to pick me up just as we were finishing our breakfast. I was expecting that, once we were inside the car, he'd tell me to be the good kid he knew I was and to try not to upset Mom ever again. Or he'd joke about me staying over at Jorgia's for a bit longer so he could save on food and water, that sort of thing. Maybe he'd even pretend things were perfectly fine and that I hadn't just egged Mom on to kill herself the day before.

Things did not go as expected.

Instead of taking me straight home, Dad brought me to a nearby ice cream place. He handed me a menu and told me to order whatever I wanted. I looked at him shrewdly as I ordered a three-scoop bowl, but he neither tried to stop me nor asked how much it was. He did take a few spoonfuls of my mint chocolate chip ice cream, which was both our favorite. We ate in silence until I was just about finished.

"Cayt," Dad said, finally breaking the ice.

"Hmm?" I asked, avoiding his gaze as I licked the bowl clean.

"I know I've made a lot of bad calls lately—"

"—What?" I said, looking up in surprise. "No, Dad—"

"—Yes, I have," Dad interrupted. "I've asked too much from you, we both know it."

I didn't answer.

"But at the same time," Dad continued, "I haven't asked enough how things have been *for* you. Or how I can help you. And I'm… I'm sorry!"

Dad's voice cracked at that last bit. He reached for me and kissed me on the forehead.

"When I think about all those times I told you to just be good or behave… like that was the reason Mom wasn't okay… I just…" Dad sputtered. "I was a terrible dad."

The sight of my dad crying touched me but freaked me out at the same time. I looked around and saw an elderly couple watching us. I gave them an apologetic smile and they smiled back.

"You weren't so bad," I teased gently, patting Dad's head. He really wasn't.

Dad pretended to strangle me for a second before letting me go with a last ruffling of my hair. After we had wiped the snot from our noses, he spoke again.

"Your Mom and I—but me, especially—we're gonna try harder," Dad continued. "I can't promise I won't need your help from time to time. But I'll do my best to look out for *all* my girls."

"We'll look out for each other," I reassured him. "Deal?"

"Deal," Dad said, grinning.

When we got home, Dad held my hand as we walked up to our front door, where Mom and Sam and our landlady were waiting for us. Sam cheered when we arrived—the only time I had ever seen her happy to see me. I pressed my forehead to the back of our landlady's hand who, after patting me on the back, then excused herself to tend to her dogs.

Mom and I faced each other awkwardly by the doorway as Dad tugged at Sam to follow him inside and leave us to our own devices. I stared at my feet, not really knowing what to say or where to start.

But I didn't have to because, before another minute could pass, Mom swept me into a hug. Not the urgent, suffocating kind that Dad had just given me half an hour ago. Rather it was soft, warm, gentle, and smelled faintly of jasmine—a perfect embrace. I had almost forgotten how it felt to be hugged by my own mother. I wrapped my arms around her as tight as I could, hoping that they could tell her all the things that I couldn't find the right words for.

Later that day, while I sat on the bench by my bedroom window, I had the strangest feeling that something was different with our room. I checked my stuff but they seemed to all be where I had left them: my small bin of filming equipment, schoolbag, the books strewn all over my side of the room, even the Super 8 on my table. I laughed at myself. I had only been gone a day—I don't think that gave me enough of an excuse to feel like a stranger in my own house.

I grabbed my phone with the intention of taking a video of the room, just so I can review it once I've properly calmed down and prove that, objectively, nothing *had* changed.

When I opened the camera app, it told me that I had run out of storage.

Boo. Clearing up space was the worst.

I opened my photo album and removed all of the footage that Jorgia and I had used for our film. I kept scrolling up, deleting photos and videos I had already posted on my social media accounts.

And that was how I found it.

I watched the video I had taken of Mom that night when she was Mom again, before she had told me about wanting to disappear. Then I scrolled for more. I found random videos of us at the kitchen, like one with Sam pestering an uncooperative

Mom to play Scrabble with her, or Mom humming while she made and eventually burned pancakes for breakfast. I even found the recording of Mom's outburst at the mall.

Watching that last video made my chest hurt at first. But, when I rewatched the others, I found myself laughing. And then my chest didn't hurt anymore.

Suddenly, I knew just what to say and how to say it.

"What are you kids up to?"

I jumped up and nearly dropped my phone when I heard Mom's voice behind me.

"Nothing!" Law, Jorgia, Sam, and I said in unison. We all laughed.

"Mmm-hmm. I've heard that before," Mom said, eyeing us suspiciously as she set down a plate of snacks on the coffee table before disappearing into their bedroom.

I went back to setting up my phone on the tripod while Law and Sam resumed boarding up our living room window with orange cellophane. Jorgia dragged a lamp from one end of the room to the other and switched it on.

I stepped back from the tripod to appreciate the effect of our set on the screen. It looked like the sun was setting outside our living room even though it wasn't even noon.

"We got it," I told my crew. "Let's roll. Just act normal, everyone."
Jorgia and Law plopped down on the sofa while Sam sat cross-legged on the floor and started painting.

With everyone in position, I pressed the red button and began recording a time lapse video. Just then, Mom and Dad stepped out of their room, dressed in going-out clothes.

"Oops," Mom said, halting mid-step. "Are we in the frame? Are we ruining your take?"

"Nah, it's fine," I said as I squeezed myself between Jorgia and Law and grabbed a cookie from the table. "Just do whatever you need to do and let the camera capture it all."

"Are you making documentaries now?" Mom asked, grabbing a cookie from the table too.

"Sort of."

"Of our house? You've been filming nothing in particular in our rooms all week."

Jorgia, Law, and I exchanged secretive looks. I just smiled at Mom and said, "Just wait and see."

"Cayt's taking a break from zombies," Dad said, winking knowingly at me before turning back to Mom. "Got everything, hun?"

Mom peered into her purse before saying, "Yes." Then she turned to Jorgia. "Are you sure your parents are okay with picking you all up, Jorg? Because we can drop you off on our way to the clinic."

Jorgia, who was halfway through a cookie just then, held up a thumb.

"S'alright Tita," she eventually managed to say. "They're on their way now."

"Let's go, hun, we don't wanna be late," Dad said, touching Mom's elbow.

Mom nodded. "Tell them thanks for doing this, Jorg. We really appreciate your family's help."

"No biggie. They like having Cayt and Sam over every week."

"What about me?" Law asked, pretending to be offended.

"Oh. Yeah, they don't mind you either," Jorgia teased him. We all laughed.

"Hey, you should leave now if you don't wanna be late for your appointment," I said, getting up from the sofa to shoo my parents away.

Once they had gone, I turned to Jorgia and Law. "Got your homework?"

They took out their phones and we giggled while watching their videos with their own moms doing the most mundane things. Jorgia's mom was reprimanding her for getting another piercing behind her back and warning her it could get infected, while Law's was teaching him how to cook rice without getting a crust.

Jorgia's Mom turned up at our driveway just as I had finished downloading the videos onto my laptop. I rushed to grab my phone from the tripod before the four of us trooped out of the house and piled into the car.

Since I first crashed at Jorgia's place, her parents had been hosting Sam and me every other Saturday while Mom went to see a counselor and Dad got a massage or had a coffee somewhere near the clinic. Today, we were going to watch an advanced screening copy of Swarog's new film *Komunidad*.

"Is this safe for Sam to watch?" I whispered to Jorgia as I grabbed the bag of popcorn from the microwave. All of Swarog's films that I've seen had been pretty violent.

"PG-13, I checked," Jorgia said, taking a handful of popcorn and shoving them into her mouth. "I think Swarog's branching out, same as you."

We went back into their living room and took our seats as Jorgia's mom started the movie. From the very beginning, my heart went out to the protagonist, this super shy guy who, one day, introduces his family to his girlfriend—a life-sized doll. While a lot of people thought it was crazy at first, the whole village decides to play along, allowing him to grow closer to them. Eventually, the main character says goodbye to his doll girlfriend and finds the courage to connect with people around him even without her.

After the movie and lunch courtesy of Jacqui (chicken roasted to perfection), Jorgia's parents dropped Sam and me off at home and told us they'd see us again the in two weeks. As I watched Jorgia and her parents drive into the distance, I got the feeling that I had a small community of my own that would help our family get better, too.

Things weren't always as reassuring as that moment, not even with Mom going to therapy or Sam and me talking with our guidance counselors or Dad opening up to us a bit more. In fact, some days were almost as bad as that one when I ran away. I'd punch and scream into my pillows, Sam would scribble her feelings onto a spare wall, Dad's hands would start trembling and itching for a smoke, and Mom would lock herself up in their room again. But having people around to support us, or even just someone to confide in, made all the difference.

FOR THE BEST

Even bad days can be good days.

My weekly meetings with Mrs. Aguirre were mostly spent playing board games and talking about how I am, how I'm dealing with school and if I'm okay with my friends, how things are at home and what help I thought I needed. But we'd always end them with me enumerating three things I was grateful for. On tough days, I realized that I was just glad enough that I could say that Mom was still hanging on to her rope—and that we all were too.

But on Tuesday, I had something to be extra grateful for. The moment I woke up, I felt like my insides were going to burst from sheer excitement. I could hardly stand still while helping Mom make champorado for breakfast.

"You know most kids wouldn't voluntarily wake up this early on a school day, right?" Mom teased.

"Well, most kids won't get the chance to meet their hero on *this* school day," I replied.

If any good had come out of the school fair, it was that our booth did make enough money to go to CineFiles. It was a week-long event but tonight, we would be attending the women filmmakers panel with Harriette Swarog. And it would be in person!

Throughout the day, it was all Jorgia and I could talk about—to the amusement and perhaps slight annoyance of Law, Alex, and Hallie (who had all gotten new dance outfits from their fair earnings). I had to admit, my mind was up in the clouds during most of my classes too and only came back down to earth for a bit when I saw Mrs. Aguirre on my way to the lunch line.

"Excited for your club trip today?" she asked when I approached her.

I beamed and nodded eagerly.

"I'm excited for you too!" Mrs. Aguirre said. "Tell me about it tomorrow when we meet?"

I nodded again. Mrs. Aguirre started walking in the direction of the faculty office and I caught up with Jorgia and the rest at the caf.

"What did Ags want?" Alex asked, peering at me.

"Oh, uh—" I began, hesitant.

"Hey, Alex, did you give a video of your mom to Cayt already?" Jorgia cut in.

"Yup, ages ago," Alex said.

"Yeah, she did," I said, smiling gratefully at Jorgia. Then, turning back to Alex, I added, "To answer your question, Ags was just reminding me about counseling tomorrow."

Alex and Hallie looked surprised for all of two seconds. Jorgia and Law seemed surprised too, but I could tell from their looks that they were proud of me for opening up. Then Alex, recovering, spoke again.

"Is she qualified for that?"

Jorgia snorted. "Of all the questions, that's the one you ask?"

"What?! I was trying to be sensitive to Cayt!"

Jorgia spent the remainder of the lunch hour abusing Alex and her obsession with political correctness, while Hallie, Law, and I came to Alex's defense, teasing Jorgia that she could use a bit of tact every now and then but most especially when eating.

On our way back to class, I walked beside Alex and told her that I wasn't sure exactly how qualified Mrs. Aguirre was but that talking to her seemed to be helping me regardless. Alex smiled and said that made her glad.

Immediately after school, Jorgia and I went to Elvira to drop off our things and change out of our uniforms for the trip.

"You're home early today," Mom said, looking startled as we walked in through the front door. She was wearing her nice cream v-neck blouse that I've been waiting to be able to borrow once puberty really started kicking in. She also had her handbag tucked under her arm.

"Just changing and grabbing a bite, Mom," I answered, dropping my backpack on the floor as I pressed my forehead onto the back of her hand. Behind me, Jorgia did the same.

"Okay, well, I'm heading out to the grocery. I left you some snacks on the table—your favorite fudge brownies."

"Cool! Thanks, Mom. We'll eat after changing," I said. I was already making my way up the spiral staircase after Jorgia.

"Aww, come here," Mom said. She walked up to me and planted a kiss on my forehead. "You girls have fun, okay? I'm so proud of you. Can't believe *my* daughter is going to meet Harriette Swarog."

"Okay, Mom! *Geroff*! Besides, we're only gonna try to ambush her after the panel so who knows if we'll actually get to meet her?"

"How do you expect to succeed with this attitude?" Mom tutted at me.

"Fine. We *will* get to talk with Harriette Swarog," I said. "Happy now?"

"Yes, as a matter of fact."

"Okay, bye then," I said, resuming the climb up the stairs.

I heard Mom say "bye" just as I entered my room.

A few minutes later, Jorgia and I were in the kitchen, stuffing our mouths (and our bags) full with all the sandwiches and brownies Mom had made. She must've been in one of her manic moods because there was almost enough to feed the whole film club.

"Are you sure," Jorgia began as she bit into her fourth brownie, "you don't wanna give Swarog a copy of our zombie movie too? I mean, they are both short."

"I know… but we need to stand out, y'know?"

"Yeah but do we wanna stand out in a bad way?" Jorgia asked, scratching her forehead.

I gasped. "You said you liked the house film!"

"I did," Jorgia sniggered. "I do!"

I pelted her with the remainder of my brownie before I stood up to clear the dishes.

"Hey! Don't crucify me for having an opinion," Jorgia said, laughing even more. Then she continued, "All I'm saying is, I'm not sure strangers will get that one the way we do."

I turned around to defend that, if anybody would get it, Swarog would. And that even if *she* didn't, what was important was what I had to say. But I completely forgot my points when I saw Jorgia's face, which seemed to have taken on the texture of bubble wrap.

"Whoa, what's wrong with you?"

"Nothing!" Jorgia said as she scratched her neck. "Just because I'm not a fan of experimental film doesn't mean something's wrong with me."

"No, look at your face!"

"What? What is it?" Jorgia asked as she shifted to one-hand scratching and grabbed my phone with her other hand. She checked her reflection in the camera. "Ohmygod, I think I'm having an allergic reaction to something!"

I looked around. We just had egg sandwiches and brownies.

"Do you have something for allergies?"

I excavated an icepack from the freezer and tossed it to Jorgia. Then I went to my parents' bathroom to get the antihistamine tablets Mom would let me take at night whenever I got the sniffles, which was often because I was still getting used to dusty Metro Manila air.

I opened the medicine cabinet and made to grab the bottle. It felt strangely light and devoid of the sound of tablets rattling against each other.

When I twisted the bottle cap open, it was empty.

That's weird, I thought. Dad always made sure we had enough of each kind of medicine because he got them at a pharmacy that was a bit farther from the house but had better prices.

I tried to call Dad on my phone, but he didn't pick up. I tried Mom, but no answer either.

I went out to the living room and found Jorgia there, looking expectantly at me as she slid the icepack all over her face and arms.

"Sorry," I said. "Looks like we're out."

"Oh no! I can't be like this when we meet Harriette! She might think I have body lice or something."

"Yeah, and what if it becomes a deadly allergic reaction?"

"That too."

"Come on, I bet someone in club will have some," I said, dragging Jorgia by the elbows towards the front door. The bus was scheduled to leave Lorenzo in less than thirty minutes!

Before we could reach the door, though, Dad walked in with Sam, who was wearing shorts over her blue leotard and white tights.

"Hey," Dad said, out of breath. "Isn't your field trip today? Why are you still here?"

"My thoughts exactly," I said, looking pointedly at Jorgia.

"Tito, I just need some allergy meds. Do you have some on you?"

"Hold on," Dad said.

We watched as he fished out a tiny pillbox from his pants pocket. He handed one to Jorgia, who popped it right in her mouth.

"Sheesh, Dad. You could've saved some for us at home," I teased him. "It's not like we're gonna drink these like vitamins."

"What're you talking about? I just replenished our medicine cabinet last night."

I sensed a change in Dad's mood as he immediately went to their bathroom. I followed him inside and watched him check the medicine cabinet.

It wasn't just the allergy meds. All the boxes and bottles were empty.

We looked at each other, eyes wide with fear.

Then I sprang into action. I sprinted out of the room and, without thinking, snatched the car keys from the counter.

"Cayt, what the heck are you doing?" Dad asked, hot on my heels. "Where's your Mom?!"

"I dunno! She said she was going to the grocery!"

"Stay here. Take Sam," Dad said, grabbing the keys from me and walking out the front door.

"No! I'm coming with you!" I shouted, jogging next to Dad and reaching our parked car at the same time as him.

Jorgia and Sam had run after us, too.

"Jorg. Take Sam, please," I said urgently and she nodded grimly, holding on tight to Sam's shoulders.

Dad and I jumped into the car and sped off.

"Where do we go?!" I asked, slapping my hands on the dashboard.

"Let's check the grocery first," Dad said.

"Nobody goes to the grocery to kill themselves!"

"It's a start!" Dad shouted, desperate. His knuckles had gone white from how hard he gripped at the steering wheel. We drove for a few minutes in silence.

Mom had said goodbye and I hadn't even noticed it.

I tried to remember what had happened earlier today—how she had made champorado and showed me exactly how to do it. How she had insisted Sam and I skip the bus today so she and Dad could drop us off on our first day back after the holidays. I pictured her tidying up the house while Dad was working on his ledgers. Then, when Dad had left to bring Sam to ballet, Mom had set about to making us enough sandwiches and brownies to last us a lifetime.

A lifetime without her.

The thought of pushing her away when she kissed me earlier today stung my eyes. Would that be Mom's last memory of me?

Or would she remember instead all the times we were at each other's throats?

I'm gonna call her," I said, blinking back my tears as we pulled up in front of the neighborhood grocery store.

I dialed Mom's number once I had leapt out of the car. I listened to the ringing at the other end of the line and silently pleaded for her to pick up.

Come on, Mom, I thought. Don't do this. Please please please, don't do this.

There was no answer. I tried again.

Dad and I split up, scouring the aisles for any sign of Mom— or a clue as to where she could possibly be.

I was walking by the produce when it happened.

Mom picked up.

"Cayt," I heard her say from the other end of the line.

"Mom!" I screamed at my phone, paying no heed to the funny looks bystanders were giving me. "Mom, where are you? Let us come get you!"

"No. That's okay. I'm good here."

"Mom, please! Just tell me where you are—" I pleaded.

"Honey, listen to me. I just wanted to say that I'm sorry."

"No! No, no, no—"

I fell on my knees, unable to hold myself up any longer.

"We tried hard, didn't we, hun? But I think it's easier this way… better," I heard Mom say. She spoke so calmly. "I know you'll manage perfectly fine without me… eventually."

Maybe Mom was right.

It would be difficult at first, but we'd be able to cope later on. Life would probably be easier without the shrink sessions and medication side effects and hospital bills and always living on edge, hiding knives and car keys and tiptoeing behind closed doors.

Easier, yes. But not better.

"I don't wanna be without you, Mom!" I wailed, clutching onto my phone for dear life.

If I were limited to these options—an easy life without Mom or a difficult one with her—there was no doubt as to which I'd rather have.

But which was better *for* Mom?

Maybe it was time to let her make her choice. And maybe she just needed to hear that it was okay for her to choose.

This could be the last time I'd ever get to talk to my mother.

"Mom? You know I just want what's best for you, right?" I sniffed. "I just want you to be happy… I love you so much."

"Thank you, Cayt. I love you too."

Then the line went dead.

PRETTY/CRAZY

There was no way to know which version of Mom I'd get each day.

But one thing was certain: No matter what, I will always be grateful for my mother.

I had often asked Mrs. Aguirre, during our previous meetings, how we could make a person want to live. What I really meant to ask was how *I* could make Mom want to live. Mrs. Aguirre never did give me an answer but I think I finally understood.

Some choices weren't mine to make. But there were still things that I *could* do.

I could choose to support and love Mom and the people in my life. And while I was at it, I could choose to love myself too, and keep count of the tiny little things that made my own life worth living.

Dad and Sam and I were hugging each other helplessly on the couch when Mom walked in through the front door late that night. I had never been so happy to see a person in my life.

We ran up to Mom and buried her in our tears and kisses. After we had surfaced for air, I whispered in Mom's ear, "I'm glad you're home."

"So am I," she whispered back.

I looked up at Mom's face. Despite the tears streaming down her cheeks, she was smiling and her eyes were full of life.

"You know you're incredible, right?" I asked her.

"That makes two of us, then," she said, kissing me on the forehead and holding me closer.

We snuggled next to each other on the sofa while Dad and Sam ordered us a late dinner.

"What happens next?" I found myself thinking aloud.

"I… don't know," Mom admitted. We sat in silence for a while.

"Maybe," I began, hesitating. "D'you think you're okay to… to go to the hospital? I mean, I just read before that that might help. For these… situations," I trailed off.

Mom didn't answer. And my insides twisted, not knowing if I had made things worse.

But after a few minutes, Mom got up and asked Dad to drive us to the hospital so we could be with her when she checked herself in. As we kissed Mom goodnight and closed the door of her hospital room behind us, I found myself smiling.

I had met my hero after all.

She wasn't some filmmaker extraordinaire. Heck, she wasn't even a perfect mother, if there were even such a thing. But she was as strong a woman as they came. Even when they could've easily overpowered her, my mom kept putting up a good fight with her own inner demons. She was a total badass.

The next morning, Dad picked Sam and me up after school so we could go straight to the hospital, only stopping on the way to get flowers for Mom. When we arrived, we listened as Mom gave us a peek inside her mind—how she herself couldn't understand the pain and confusion and anger and helplessness she often felt even if she knew for a fact that she loved and was grateful for us. How she had some regrets in her past life, and how she felt a lot of pressure in the present. And all of those, together with her grief over Miggy and the isolation during the past few years, may have been why she kept thinking ending her life was the only good option left to her.

Sam gave Mom a bear hug.

"I'm sorry you felt awful, Mom… But I'm really happy you're with us now."

It was kind of a surprise how, despite her age and limited vocabulary, Sam had captured exactly how I, too, felt.

Once Mom had been discharged, we were at a bit of a loss as to how we should go about things. What's the first thing you should do when your mother comes home from treatment for an attempt on her life? We had been through it before and learned the long and hard way that sweeping the issue under the rug and trying to pretend everything was okay didn't work all that well.

So we tried a different approach.

We told a few more of the people who mattered—Lola and Ate Fe, close relatives and friends, our teachers, and even our landlady—the gist of what we were going through and how we hoped we could count on them for support and patience and understanding.

Then we made our own happy/sad scale and taped it to the fridge. Every day, we'd place our face magnets somewhere along the scale to gauge how we were feeling at that moment. Mom's doctor said it was important to be self-aware so we knew how we could help ourselves. But I thought it was also pretty useful because the scale made it easier to know how we could help each other. Like, if Sam's magnet was on the really sad end, I'd offer to split my pack of Yakult with her as we talked about stuff. I just had to make sure she didn't keep doing that just to get my Yakult.

It felt like a small victory to see that, as the weeks passed by, Mom's magnet moved steadily towards the right-hand side of the scale.

One week before school ended, I felt like sliding down my magnet to the rightmost side myself. Mrs. Aguirre had just congratulated me for making the honor roll.

"Can't wait to tell Mom!" I told Jorgia as we made our way past the Lorenzo gates. "Hey, your grades are almost there too. I bet you could make it next year."

"No thanks! I like being average. It helps me manage the pressure."

"Sometimes I don't know if you're crazy or a genius," I said, laughing.

"Probably both. And I don't need to be on honors to prove that!"

Jacqui picked Jorgia and me up so she could drive us to Cinema Paradiso for our volunteer shift. Throughout the ride, the three of us debated about the rest of the things we should avoid if we were to follow Jorgia's logic, like composing a wicked score, winning an Oscar, or getting a boyfriend even. The debate continued even after Jacqui had dropped us off and only ended when I had taken my seat behind the ticket booth and Jorgia had disappeared into the AV room.

Just a few minutes later, Mom showed up at the booth.

"Two tickets for whatever the next film is going to be, please," she said.

"Mom! You're early!"

Every Friday, Mom would pick me up in a cab after my three-hour shift at Paradiso, on the way home from her bipolar support group meetings. She had found a small circle that met regularly and, since her doctor had encouraged her to keep to a routine, Mom joined the group. She said it was a nice addition to her new part-time remote job subtitling movies.

So far, I had to agree. Mom would often tell us how reassuring it was to know other people had gone through what she had—and actually found joy in soldiering on. Most days, anyway.

Did I fear that, in the sliver of time between support group and Paradiso, when she was alone, she could hoard tablets again at the nearest drugstore?

Sure I did. Almost every freakin' time.

But I believed in Mom. And the rest of us were doing our best too. So the only thing left for me to do was to trust and just hope for the best.

I smiled at the sight of Mom in front of me, glad that hope did not disappoint me today.

"What happened to BP? They didn't cancel, did they?" I asked.

"Don't worry. They didn't," Mom said, slipping her hand through the window so she could put it over mine. "But there were only three of us so we finished pretty fast."

I exhaled, relieved.

"Anyway, didn't you say we should watch a movie today, just you and me, like the old times?" Mom reminded me.

"Yes, I did," the sense of relief quickly evaporating as I answered.

After re-editing the house movie for the nth time, I had planned on showing Mom the new cut by inserting it between the trailers and the main feature, which was this really good local heist comedy. But what I had not planned on was her arriving half an hour early. Jorgia was still rendering!

I looked around desperately and my eyes landed on the newly reopened snack bar.

"Hey, Mom? What's a movie without snacks, right? Why don't you grab some while I get somebody to take my place here?"

"Hmm, okay," Mom said before sauntering to the snack bar at the end of the hallway.

I ran to the AV room.

"She's here! Is it done yet?"

"What do you mean 'she's here?' It's only four-thirty!"

"I know that! *Isitdoneyet*?!"

Jorgia turned her laptop towards me and showed me the screen. Three more long minutes to finish rendering. Add to that the time she needed to check the video then upload it to the queue and I'd need to stall for a full seven minutes. Minimum.

I went out and saw that Mom was about to walk past the curtains and into the theater. I couldn't let that happen—she'd see our surprise before it was ready!

"MOM!" I yelled.

A handful of other moviegoers who looked like they were in their late teens stared at me like I was crazy. But I didn't care. I jogged up to Mom, who looked very concerned at my apparent lack of social graces.

"Is something wrong, Cayt?"

"No," I said, shaking my head in my best attempt to display normalcy. "Oh, hey! What snacks did you get? 'Coz I had my eye on the—"

"Mint Oreos and caramel popcorn," Mom answered. "Of course."

For a moment, I forgot that I was supposed to be stalling. How nice was it to have somebody remember all your favorite stuff, right?

"Let's sit so we can dig in," Mom said, turning towards the curtains once more.

"Actually," I said, grabbing her by the arms, "I think I'm in a barbecue flavor kind of mood. Let's see if they have any."

I steered Mom towards the snack bar where she immediately grabbed a bag of Chippy and paid for it. I checked my watch. It hasn't even been three minutes yet.

"Okay, let's go," Mom said.

"Wait! How about a Yakult?"

"Cayt Valerie," Mom said, looking very stern. Was she on to me?

"*Yeees*?" I answered slowly.

"I'm sure you're aware that the snacks here cost twice as much as they would in the supermarket. Just because it's not your money and we're now a two-income household, doesn't mean you can just spend without a care."

"Dad, is that you?" I teased.

"How dare you?" Mom punched my arm playfully. "Do you think your Dad would've even agreed to get you one thing here?"

I laughed. "He would've probably run two blocks to buy a bag of chips from a *sari-sari.*"

"No doubt," Mom said, doubling over. "And you know he hates cardio! Now come on and don't ask for more treats."

"Okay, okay, just wait a sec," I said as I bent down to re-tie my shoelaces, taking my time but keeping an eye on Mom's foot in case it walked away.

As I straightened myself up, I noticed that the snack bar had small packs of round biscuits with rainbow-colored meringue on top. They were the same ones that Mrs. Aguirre had given us on the first day back. I took it and showed it to my Mom.

"Oh! Iced Gems! I loved these as a kid," she said. "There were so many colors, I used to think no two were alike."

It had been a while back, but I realized I never had a chance to tell Mom about my first day in Lorenzo.

"Mrs. Aguirre gave us all one of these at the start of school," I told her as I turned over the pack in my hand, watching how the little biscuits moved around inside when I shook it. "She gave us a bunch of stuff, actually, and said that each of them meant something."

I got what the eraser and the sticker of her face was for. And I guess the gum had something to do with us sticking together or maybe expanding ourselves? I dunno. One of those.

"So what were the biscuits for?" Mom asked.

"Hmm. Not sure actually."

"Maybe it means you're all gems," Mom suggested.

"Sure, maybe…"

"Well, I guess we can splurge on just one more thing," Mom said, winking at me before she handed the biscuits and some money to the cashier. "You never know if eating them might help you figure it out."

"Thanks, Mom," I said as I fished out a handful of biscuits from the pack she had just opened and was offering to me. The meringue bit had a mild sweetness, and the biscuit had just the right amount of crunch. It was really good.

Mom and I smiled at each other as we finished the bag even before we got to the curtains that led to the theater.

Whatever they meant, I guess I still had time to figure it out, I thought with a shrug. As we ushered ourselves inside, I turned around in the direction of the AV room and saw Jorgia peeking through a gap in the door, giving me the thumbs up.

Everything would be alright.

Mom and I eagerly watched the trailers before the movie, debating about which one we should see next. I flat out refused to see the film that had a running time of ten hours, even though she argued that it would be a cinematic masterpiece— and a Filipino production nonetheless.

"No, Mom. I'm just a teenager with a limited attention span— and I draw the line at four."

"Oh, come on, Cayt—!"

"Spending a whole day watching *a* movie?"

Mom paused at what I said.

"Actually, you're right, that is pretty crazy… and I should know."

I giggled.

Just then, a familiar opening billboard started playing on the screen. After a few seconds, the title card dissolved to make way for a wide shot of our living room, my family and friends coming and going in the bright morning light. I had shot images of our home to reflect my relationship with my mother: from my birth and "normal" childhood, to the difficult period after the loss of

Miggy, to this day when we're still trying to figure things out, and to how I hoped the days to come would be like. But I used audio from my own videos of Mom (including a few when she was angry or sad) and those of Sam's and my friends', and even a conversation between Dad and my grandmother, splicing and rearranging the voice clips until they matched the scenes.

"They sound familiar," Mom whispered when she heard our voices.

From slow and calm and bright, the room became fierce and buzzing and orange, then dark and still, then almost chaotic until, finally, it was golden and serene.

After a minute and a half, the screen faded to black. When my dedication, "For Mom," flashed for a brief second, I heard Mom draw a sharp breath beside me. She squeezed my hand.

"It's beautiful, Cayt," she whispered to me again, her eyes shining bright in the dark theater.

"Thank you, Mom," I said.

I think I'll always enjoy watching and making movies about zombies and the undead. But I'll always be grateful for the chance to honor someone who—no matter what happened in the future—would always live on.

When the school year first started, I mourned for my closeness with Mom. I had always thought that being close to each other meant you got along ninety-nine percent of the time and never had any grievances or fights with one another. That you could sit at a table together and talk for hours without ever running out of things to laugh about. Certainly, being close meant you didn't scream at the other person to get lost or kill themselves, right?

But now I knew that being close to each other meant you could disagree and be different from one another. You could tell the other person when you're not okay—or even when you have a problem with them, though preferably in a calm manner. You could let them inside your occasionally troubled mind and they'd thank you for being honest and not run away from you. You could sometimes feel anger or shame or disappointment or frustration with them—but still know at the end of the day that you love them, and that they love you.

Other families might find it weird and crazy, but this was our normal now. And when I really thought about it—the crazy and the bad days, the days when all of our magnets teetered dangerously towards the sad end—well, they made the good even better.

Mom laced her fingers with mine as the movie started. And just like that, I knew that our fates were tied together.

Not necessarily in the sense that if she dipped again, I would too. But that it was exactly because of the events of our past together that I had a deeper appreciation for our present now. That I was who I am and who I will be—not in spite of her—but because of her. And that could actually be good.

Mom and I sat side by side in Paradiso, savoring every second together until the house lights went back on, and the end credits began to roll.

ABOUT THE AUTHOR

Katrina Martin was a fellow at the 3rd Amelia Lapeña Bonifacio Writers Workshop (The Novel) and a finalist in PBBY - Scholastic Asia's You Write to Me, I'll Write to You manuscript competition in 2017. Born and raised in Manila, she completed her BS in Nursing at the University of the Philippines Manila and her MA in Creative Writing at the University of the Philippines Diliman. Kat has written professionally for television, film, and the global social sector. At Home with Crazy is her first novel.

This book's typeface is set using
Minion Pro and Chalkduster.
Minion Pro is designed by
Robert Slimbach and was released
in 1990. The typeface is ideal for use
in books, newsletters, and packaging
because of its classical and elegant
aesthetic as well as its functional
qualities that make the text type
highly readable.

Chalkduster is a font released by Apple
in 2003 to apply chalk writing style.

The cover art is illustrated by
Angela Taguiang. It depicts Cayt's face
on the right, and her mother's on the
left. Their faces form a silhouette of a
house, inspired by the title of the novel.